Something BLUE

Something Blue

HANNAH RIO

Copyright © 2024 by Hannah Rio

All rights reserved.

No part of this book may be reproduced in any form or by any electronic or mechanical means, including information storage and retrieval systems, without written permission from the author, except for the use of brief quotations in a book review.

A Note From Hannah

SOME HANNAH RIO TITLES MAY CONTAIN TRIGGERS, PLEASE READ WITH CAUTION, AND LOOK AFTER YOUR MENTAL HEALTH.

Sign up to her newsletter here:
subscribepage.io/NKn98Z

CHAPTER ONE
Neve

I keep glancing over at the wall clock, with its pearl inlaid face and elegant silver hands ticking away the time. Second by second, my anxiety is growing worse.

I glance up at the mirror in front of me - looking past my reflection towards my best friend, Dalila Vece.

"Is there any sign of him yet?" I ask tensely.

"Not yet, but he'll be here. He got held up somewhere." She reassures me - for the hundredth time. She has been my best friend for years. Our families have been tangled together in a kind of weird way, but despite all of that, she and I got on like a house on fire from the first moment we met.

I adore her and if she wasn't here right now, I'd be losing my mind.

"He's always so careful about time." I sigh.

It's not like Damion to be late for anything.

Especially not our wedding.

The makeup artist and hair lady are fussing around me, making me look *perfect*. Everything has to be perfect, according to my father. The perfect dress, the perfect venue, perfect food, and perfect decor - but nothing is perfect unless the groom shows up.

I shift on the dressing table chair and pull my mouth tight.

"Honey, you need to relax, or I can't do your makeup." The girl complains, speaking gently, but is definitely annoyed with me. I've been fidgeting the whole time. She's had to fix makeup splodges twice already. I can't believe Damion isn't here yet.

We've been engaged for about four months. It wasn't really a choice - more of a convenience. My father requires that I marry someone with status, money, and power. All of which Damion's family has. Upstanding citizens who will reflect well on my father.

And Damion and I get on well enough, I can deal with him as my husband. It's also the perfect way for me to escape my father's overbearing rules.

Rules about what I may wear. Rules about where I may go. Rules about how I speak and every single choice I make.

Being a politician's daughter is not all it's cut out to be. I've been made aware of the media my entire life. Hyper perfection is the only option. My father's campaign is running smoothly at the moment - with the help of some dodgy investors - but the media rules our lives.

So, Damion was chosen to be my husband because he's a good fit for the image our family needs.

But where the hell is he? *It's our wedding day.*

"Dalila." I turn around in my seat and the makeup artist sighs loudly. I wave her away from me, my annoyance trumping hers. She steps back and fidgets with her brushes to cover the redness of her cheeks.

"Neve?" Dalila says, smiling, trying to maintain a cool, positive outlook, although I am falling apart at the seams.

"Did you try calling him again?" I ask, standing up because I need to pace around.

"I've been calling, but his phone is off. Look - honey, he's obviously stuck somewhere, he forgot to charge his phone, it's probably something so silly - but he will be here. We need to get you ready. Ok?"

"And my brother? Did he go check Damion's apartment?"

"He said he was going to send someone. He didn't want to leave the wedding and cause suspicion."

I sigh and close my eyes for a moment, fighting tears that will completely ruin the makeup that I really don't want to sit for anymore. "Ok. Ok. Ok." I say quietly.

Get ready - focus on that. By the time you're done, he will be here.

I sit down and face the mirror again. My bright blue eyes are staring back at me - filled with concern. What if he got cold feet? *Impossible*. He knows this marriage is important. Not only to us - but to both families. He lives under the strain of the media just as much as I do. He wouldn't cause a scene like this. No. Something has happened. I just hope it's not serious, and he gets here on time.

The hairdresser pins the last glittering crystal into my curled, braided, pinned up hair and I turn my head to the side to admire the overall effect. It's going to be an absolute nightmare to get that out before I go to bed, but my pale blonde hair looks gorgeous. She holds a mirror up behind me and I nod. The makeup artist touches a dash of gloss to my full caramel tinted lips, then they both step away from me.

"Thank goodness." I huff when the girls announce my hair and makeup are *done*.

I stand up and hurry over to Dalila, who has unhooked my dress from the cupboard where it was hanging. She slides the hanger out from the high halter neck and drapes the dress over her arm. "You ready to tango yourself into this thing?" She laughs.

Trying on the dress was a nightmare. It's so fitted around the bodice and up over my chest and they still tailored it even tighter to fit more snugly against my body - it's like a corset on steroids. But it is beautiful. Like ridiculously beautiful. Personally, I would have chosen a low-cut neckline, but my father wants pristine elegance, and apparently cleavage isn't allowed. For a dress 'within the rules' I am super excited to wear this one.

I wish the excitement wasn't tainted by so much stress.

I slide the white silk gown off my shoulders. The little 'bride' embroidered label with my name beneath it makes me frown. I catch a glimpse of myself in the long hotel room mirror. All white lace lingerie - looking super hot for my wedding night - but where is the groom?

"He'll be here." She says, noticing my face.

"I have a bad feeling." I mutter, stepping into the dress while Dalila holds it open for me. She starts to tug it up over my hips while I do little hops and breathe in a lot until it's up over my chest and she has hooked the halter section around my neck.

"Ok, now for the hard part." She laughs, tugging at the braided cord that pulls it even tighter.

"Ugh." I gasp and hold on to one of the bedposts.

"Breathe in." She giggles, tugging again.

"I *am breathing in.*" I crack up laughing as she literally has to throw me around to get the dress on properly.

Fifteen minutes later we are both laughing and I'm gently dabbing perspiration off my forehead and hoping I haven't messed up my makeup - again.

"You are fucking *gorgeous.*" Dalila says with a massive smile.

A knock at the hotel room door has us both turning towards it.

"Come in." I say, hoping like hell that someone is here to tell me Damion has arrived.

My father walks into the room with Luke following close behind, head to toe dapper in their black tuxedos with pale olive-green pocket squares. I didn't choose olive green as my wedding accent color. The wedding planner did - she said it was the most appealing color for media coverage. Voted the top color on some social media poll. Whatever. Green it is.

"My angel, my sweetheart, you look absolutely perfect." My father says, walking towards us with his arms out. There's that perfect word again.

"Is Damion here?" I ask tensely.

Luke stands near the door looking like security instead of my brother.

"Don't you even worry about it. He'll be here." My father says, but I can see how stressed he is. Not that there is ever a time when he isn't stressed.

"Dad." I complain, but he holds his hand in the air to cut me off.

"He'll be here. You are going to carry on, do your part, and by the time the music plays, he *will be here*." He says sternly. I nod tightly. I don't have the same confidence. Something is wrong.

My father places his finger beneath my chin and turns my face from side to side to look at me.

"Perfect." He says. "Now remember, keep your head held high. Don't look at the floor when you walk. Walk slowly and elegantly, no marching down the aisle. Speak clearly and loudly, but don't shout when you say your vows. Always make sure your body is tilted towards a camera, like they showed you in PR training."

"Dad." I huff. "Please, I'm stressed enough as it is."

He glares at me, and I bite my lip. No one talks back to my father. Especially not me.

"There will be a reporter sitting with a cameraman in the front row. That news site has exclusive rights to the first interview after the wedding, so always favor them when you face the crowd." He says.

I nod.

I can't believe that even on my wedding day, I don't get to relax and enjoy it. Never mind the fact that my husband-to-be is a no show so far - I have to think about how I stand, how I walk, where I look - I can't enjoy myself.

My father glances at his watch.

"It's time. You can head down to the church." He says coldly and walks away without another word of reassurance or even a sentimental father-daughter moment like I was hoping for. He gestures for my brother to follow him and quickly they are both gone.

I glance at Dalila, and she can instantly see the tears burning at the back of my eyes. She steps forward and wraps her arms around me, hugging me, not disturbing any of my wedding-outfit-vibes.

"It's going to be ok." She whispers against my ear.

I love her. She's amazing. I need her more than she knows.

It's so strange how our families came to be acquainted.

Her family - dodgy Italian mafia *'business'* men - make exceptionally large contributions to my father's political campaigns. Now I know, because I'm not a freaking moron, that they make these donations in order to gain control for their own family. Nothing without something in return. And my father benefits from the sizable contributions.

Dalila and I don't care about any of that. We just get on. That's all. Nothing else matters.

Her entire family is here at my wedding - waiting somewhere outside.

"Ready?" she asks, handing me a bunch of white lilies and giant monstera leaves.

A gorgeous bouquet for my gorgeous wedding.

I nod, clenching my jaw.

"Don't forget to smile." she says in a deep voice, mocking my father.

I giggle and smile a genuine smile.

Thank goodness for Dalila.

She walks with me towards the elevator, and we ride down together. The church is in the hotel, a gorgeous, oversized, way too expensive package deal. I guess when you have over a thousand people at your wedding, you don't want to have to maneuver them from one venue to another. All in one makes sense.

The guests are busy moving from the pre-drinks and snacks room and into the church. Dalila tugs me to the side so no one sees my dress or me.

She grins and waves at people as they walk past while I hide behind the corner.

"Oh, my word - I forgot my phone upstairs. I

wanted to take photos." She whines, pouting sadly.

"Run. You can make it. I won't go anywhere, I promise." I laugh.

"You sure?"

"Sure. Go."

Dalila bolts off, her bridesmaid dress flowing out behind her. The olive green suits her tanned skin and brings out her bright green eyes. Her hair used to be blonde, dyed to annoy her father, but it's dark now, pinned up and looking gorgeous.

I watch her until she's out of sight. I sigh and lean against the wall, still hiding.

I hear people chatting as they walk past. Most of them asking where the groom is.

My heart tightens and my stomach knots.

"Dalila should bring her down any second." Masaccio remarks. I recognize his voice anywhere. Dalila's oldest brother. Celso huffs in response. A bitter sort of laugh that makes my skin tingle with a warning. "Not much of a wedding without the groom." Celso remarks with amusement in his voice.

I peek around the corner and watch them. Masaccio turns to Celso. His eyes are dark with distrust. "What did you do, Celso?" he whispers, a dark, hushed accusation.

"Nothing." Celso says loudly, lifting his hands in the air in defense and smiling broadly.

Celso is the youngest of Dalila's brothers. At twenty-nine, he is only six years older than I am. And he's fucking hot. Like super fucking hot. But totally off limits. Dalila made me swear on more than one occasion to never get involved with any of her brothers because it might ruin our friendship. I've respected that, but that doesn't mean I haven't perved Celso on more than one occasion.

The problem is - he's dangerous.

I can see it a mile away. He's unpredictable, always gets his own way - and never has to take responsibility for any of the things he does. And he does some pretty fucked up shit.

His father always covers for him.

And now Masaccio is questioning him about what he did to cause Damion to be late for his own wedding.

My stomach churns. *Was Celso involved?*

My heart rate increases and a dizzy wave of nausea rushes through me.

Surely not - why would he do something to mess up my wedding? What would he have to gain from that?

Maybe just pleasure - at someone else's suffering? He is that twisted.

"Hey, I'm back." Dalila says, a little out of breath. These stilettos are *not* made for running. She laughs, clutching her phone in her hand. "Oh, my goodness, you are so pale. What happened?" she asks, worried.

I shake my head. "It's ok. Just nerves."

CHAPTER TWO
Celso

The wedding is delayed. They're running behind schedule, but it's not a surprise. The groom hasn't shown up.

Which is also no surprise.

I smirk as we settle into the wooden seats lined up in a massive semi-circle around the altar. The altar where Damion Levine is supposed to be waiting for his bride.

Masaccio elbows me and throws me an angry glare. "Stop smiling. It looks fucked up."

"Oh please, look around you. Tons of people are smiling." I huff.

Masaccio stares at me, his eyes piercing into mine. "Just say it, Celso - did you do something?" he demands, a harsh whisper.

I chuckle. "You're so quick to accuse me, Mas. Why in the world would I want to mess up Neve's wedding? She's our sister's best friend."

Mas growls angrily. "We both know why."

I turn my face forward, away from him and his foul mood.

I'm in a great mood today. It's a gorgeous day for a wedding to fall apart. Especially when it's a wedding that should never have taken place to begin with. I told Neve she belonged to me. I've told her more than once. She brushes it off and plays me down - but it's time she realized how serious I am about this.

In fact, that she even thought she had a right to marry someone else - it infuriates me. It causes anger to bubble and boil inside me.

I clench my jaw, not wanting to get worked up. Things are fine. I made sure they were fine.

There will be no wedding.

The pre-ceremony party was fun, though. I enjoyed the whiskey and the rather exquisite food selection. Tasters carried around by arrogant servers in black and white penguin suits.

This is all a waste of time, but I have to go with the flow until they figure out the groom really isn't coming.

I fold my arms across my chest and sigh quietly, turning my wrist towards my face so I can see the time.

Dalila leans over the chair in front of us. "Guys, he's still not here yet. Neve is going crazy. I'm really worried, but I'm trying to keep her calm."

"Where is she?" I ask, wanting to see her.

"She's waiting outside the church, but seriously, I don't know what to do—"

Masaccio stands up. He glances backwards down the rows and rows of guests, all starting to grow impatient. "Shit. There are so many people here." He sighs.

"I want to go look in his hotel room, but can one of you stand with Neve?" Dalila asks tightly.

"I'll stay with her. Mas, go with Dalila." I suggest.

Mas glares at me with his jaw clenched but doesn't say anything suggestive of my involvement. He wouldn't want to upset our little sister.

"Fine. Let's go." He mutters under his breath.

We make our way out of our seats and into the aisle, walking quickly out of the church.

Neve is standing in the little foyer area, near a stained-glass window that looks out into the garden behind the giant hotel. She looks like an angel with the colorful light of the window splashing over her. It's me she should be marrying. Not some random asshole who doesn't deserve her. She's mine. She's been mine since the second I set my eyes on her.

Mas and Dalila hurry away to search Damion's hotel room.

I wander slowly over to Neve, my eyes tracing over her gorgeous body, the tight fit of her wedding dress sculpting perfectly over her small waist and wide hips.

"You are beautiful enough to break a hundred

hearts tonight." I say, and she spins around in fright, her eyes wide when they meet mine.

Fuck.

She is exquisite.

I shove my hands into my pockets and smile at her with my head tilted to the side. "Exquisite." I say, winking at her.

She glares up at me, a foot shorter than me, but looking fierce enough to take me down. Not that she could. But I'd love for her to try. I chuckle to myself.

"*What* is so funny?" She snaps.

"Nothing." I shrug. "I heard you needed a groom. I'd love to take over from the idiot who stood you up." I take a step closer to her and she stiffens.

I can smell her perfume. Delicate, a hint of lemon. It's fresh and enticing.

"He didn't stand me up. He would never do that." She mutters, quiet and tense, with my eyes locked onto her like a wolf hunting a tiny little rabbit.

She shudders as though something has run up her spine.

She closes her eyes and shakes her head, clearing her mind, shifting her thoughts.

"What's the time?" She demands. Her voice changed, no longer a meek whisper.

"Almost a quarter to five."

I watch her swallow hard and the glittering shadow of tears that spring to her eyes.

"Five?" she mumbles. "The wedding was supposed to start at three thirty."

She looks around as though she's trying to find an escape and I step closer and reach out my hand, running it down her back, my fingers tracing over her body. She's frozen, so I reach up and brush one of her tears away with the pad of my thumb.

"He'll be here." I reassure her, knowing I'm lying to her. I dip my thumb into my mouth and taste her tears.

Salty, sweet tears from the woman who belongs to me.

She steps back, away from me, throwing me a foul glare. "Don't touch me, Celso." She sounds more flustered than offended. Her breath hitched slightly.

Mm. I'd love to know what else she tastes like.

"He's not there." Dalila's voice comes from behind me, and Neve's face tightens.

"What is going on?" She whispers. "All those people in there—" She glances towards the church doors and clenches her fist around the flowers she's holding in one hand, slung low against her side as though they are nothing but a burden at this point.

"Isn't there anything we can do?" Neve asks Mas.

"I can't trace his number with his phone being off." He shrugs.

It wouldn't help. I smile inwardly.

"Is there some way we can—"

"Where the fucking hell is he?" Franco Greco's voice is a booming annoyance in my ears. An arrogant man who looks down on my family, although we are the only reason he can afford to run his political campaigns. He views himself as high society and us as mafia scum - a necessary evil in his plans for ultimate power.

"No one knows, daddy. Please keep your voice down." Neve moans.

"I will kill this boy. How dare he embarrass us like this." Greco snarls, his fists clenched and his jaw muscles tensing as he chews away at his own teeth in agitation.

"Embarrassing?" Neve spits. "You're *embarrassed*? That's *all*? Nothing about how your *daughter* feels on her wedding day - nothing about me - no care in the entire world?" She's furious and taking it all out on her father.

"Neve, be quiet. We don't want the reporters hearing." Greco warns her.

"Oh, the *tragedy*, if a reporter hears that *I'm upset about the fact that my fiancé has not shown up to marry me while I stand here in this straight jacket of a dress, hardly able to breathe.*" She shouts.

Her father grabs her arm and drags her further away from the church doors, towards the steps, and out into a small indoor garden area.

We follow, all of us, Dalila looking panicked and wanting to help her friend. Mas looking like he might be ready to break up a fight - and me - well, I want to know what's going to happen next.

But if Greco doesn't take his hands off Neve soon - he will be answering to me.

Father and daughter continue to argue under whispered harsh breath. Neve's cheeks are growing redder by the second, and her eyes are flooding with tears. She throws her hands in the air in exasperation and glares at her father with pure horror.

"You want me to do what?" she asks in disbelief.

"I want you to go into the church and address the guests. Tell them you are grateful they came out here, and they can please still enjoy the reception food and drink, otherwise it will go to waste."

"Dad, I can't." She stammers. "I can't do that." Tears are streaking down her cheeks.

"I'll do it." Dalila steps forward. "As the maid of honor, it makes sense for me to do it—"

She looks hopefully at Greco, who sneers and drags his eyes up and down over her in disapproval. This man better watch himself. He is getting on my last nerve.

Mas sighs, running his hand through his hair. "I'll stand with you." He says to Dalila.

"Fine." Greco snaps and storms off without another word.

Dalila gently touches Neve's arm. "I'm so sorry." She whispers.

Neve shakes her head, unable to speak. Her throat tightening with tears. Tears wasted on another man. A man she should never have been involved with.

I hate to see her broken like this. But I warned her.

"It's ok." She finally mutters and Dalila smiles tightly before glancing at Mas. My brother and sister leave the garden. And now I am alone with Neve again.

She doesn't seem to notice that I'm here.

I take my time watching her in her assumed privacy. She is crying a little more freely now but trying to get it under control.

Wiping her fingers underneath her eyes to stop the makeup from running, she takes a deep breath and holds it in. Counting.

…three…four… five. She lets it out.

Fuck. She is beautiful.

Literally the most gorgeous woman on the planet.

"Neve." I say gently, and she spins around with her eyes wide and horrified.

"I thought you left." She snaps, quickly brushing her hand across her face and pushing her shoulders back.

"You're allowed to show emotion. You are human." I say, walking around her, admiring every inch of her.

She scrunches her nose and turns her head to follow me with her eyes.

"I need to be alone, Celso." She sighs. "Can't you respect that, please."

I sneer. When will she understand she belongs to me?

"Fine. But when you are ready - I will be waiting for you."

"Waiting for what?" She sighs, annoyed. I pause behind her, and step closer so that our bodies are touching.

"You know exactly what, Neve." I say darkly, my voice low, my mouth pressed against her ear as I stand with my chest up against her back.

For a second, she leans into me, her breath catches in her throat and her lip's part. The sight of her minute submission sends wild currents of electricity rushing through me.

As quickly as she gave in, she regains herself and steps forward.

She won't look at me. But I saw what I needed to see.

"See you soon, Neve." I whisper and walk out of the garden to leave her grieving over her spoiled wedding day.

CHAPTER THREE
Neve

Suddenly, I'm completely and utterly alone in the little garden.

Gentle flowing water features like miniature waterfalls flow over a rock wall to my left. To my right is a garden made up of orchids - magnificent, unusual colors spread across the ornate and carefully designed landscape.

It's a perfectly designed secret garden. We were going to have some of our wedding photographs taken in here.

My heart splinters.

It's not only the fact that Damion didn't arrive - it's also my father. How cruel and heartless he can be, even in moments like this. Moments when a daughter would really need her father.

A shiver runs down my spine and I turn quickly, half expecting Celso to still be there watching me. He makes me so nervous. The dangerous look in his gorgeous eyes. The way he acts like he has a right to do whatever he pleases whenever he pleases, as though there are no consequences for him.

He scares me a little. And that turns me on a little. Which pisses me off a little.

I sigh loudly, brushing away the last tear I will allow myself to cry before I plaster the bravest expression onto my face and head out into the reception area to face one million questions and looks of pathetic empathy and pity from everyone who glances in my direction.

I'm mortified.

But also really worried about what has happened to Damion.

I give myself a five-minute limit and when the time is up, I brush my hands over my dress and lift my head high.

Then I step out of the garden and into the foyer leading to the church.

I practically collapse in relief when I see Dalila waiting there for me.

"Please, stay with me." I whisper, leaning close to her. "My father will be out appeasing the reporters, and I don't want to be alone in this crowd."

Dalila laughs a mischievous little snort. "Oh honey, there is no way we are going to the reception so that you can be entertainment for these vultures."

"My father said—"

"Yes, yes - I heard what your dad said, but let's be honest - this sucks balls. I have no idea how you are holding yourself together so elegantly. You don't need *that*—" she gestures towards the crowded passage the leads to the reception venue. People are already gawking at me.

I bite at my lower lip.

We stand quietly to the side, Dalila smiling and nodding at the guests as they flood from the church into the other venue. She is acting as a shield between them and me.

"Ready?" she asks when the crowd starts to thin out.

"For what?" I ask in confusion.

"*Now*." She grins, grabbing my hand as she tugs me across the open space and into an elevator. She slams her fingers against the button until the door closes.

"Dalila—" I can't help but grin too. "What are you up to?"

"After party." She raises one of her brows and the elevator rides up to what was supposed to be my honeymoon suite that I had booked for this evening.

On the top floor Dalila tugs me towards the best room in the entire hotel. It's the penthouse. She swipes the keycard that she obviously found in all my belongings and pushes the door open.

It's gorgeous.

The room is massive, as big as an apartment, and the views are shockingly good. On the kitchen counter is a basket of champagne, chocolate, cheese and biscuits and a wide assortment of other snacks.

She walks straight over to it and grabs one of the champagne bottles.

"He might have made the biggest mistake in his life by ditching you, but that doesn't mean we can't party." She grins, twisting the cork.

Giving in I pick up the two crystal champagne glasses, jumping a little when the cork shoots out in a loud pop, holding them towards Dalila so she can pour glittering gold champagne for us.

"To the man - who clearly didn't deserve you." She smiles, lifting her glass.

I sip my champagne, a little dry for my taste, but who cares?

My heart clenches when I think of how badly today went. I down the rest of what's in my glass.

"Wow. Ok. I'll put the other two bottles in the fridge to chill." Dalila says, first topping my glass up.

I wander over to the balcony and tug the glass doors open to let in a gentle afternoon breeze. Taking a deep breath, I close my eyes and tell myself everything is going to be ok.

I down the second glass of champagne.

"Oh, fuck it." Dalila laughs, carrying the bottle out to the balcony to stand with me.

Hours later we are both beyond tipsy. Laughing at nothing, lying stretched out on the fluffy white carpet in the living room and staring at the crystal chandelier above our heads.

"Do you want to know something funny?" I say, slurring my words a little.

"I want to know how you are still breathing in that wedding dress - but sure - something funny - go for it." Dalila snickers.

"When he didn't show up - at first, I was horrified. Embarrassed, rejected, feeling like everyone was judging me." I roll onto my stomach so that I can sip my champagne.

"And now?" She asks.

"Well - I cried about it - because that's the normal thing to do, but when I was talking to your brother and something he said made me realize - *I was relieved.*"

"Huh?" She splutters, rolling onto her stomach as well, kicking her legs up behind herself.

"What did my brother say? What do you mean?"

"Pfft. I can't remember what he said - but I was *relieved*, Dalila. And now even *more* so since I've got over the shock of it all. I didn't want to marry Damion. He's an amazing person, a good guy, but like - boring."

I shrug.

"Most arranged marriages are like that. A marriage of convenience."

"Not yours." I tilt my head to the side and the room spins.

"I got lucky."

"I want to get lucky."

A knock on the door makes us both jump and laugh, Dalila spills champagne on the carpet and brushes her hand across it to hide it, still giggling.

The door pushes open and in walks Mas and Celso.

Mas looks angry as he stares down at the two drunkest girls, I think he's seen in a while.

"What are you doing?" He sighs, running his hand through his hair and shaking his head. "Dalila, people have been asking where the bride is."

"Well—" She huffs indignantly. "They *should* be asking where the *groom* is."

Celso laughs, a deep sexy sound that rumbles through me and I grin at him in my rather tipsy state.

Fuck. He's even hotter than before. When did that happen?

I shift myself and sit up, my legs getting tangled in the dress, so I hitch it up higher giving myself more space to move.

Celso's eyes take me in hungrily and I smirk. He thinks I'm hot. I can see it all over his face.

He's always wanted me. He's told me more than once.

But I promised my friend I'd never date her brothers. And besides - *it's Celso*. He's not the kind of guy you date. Dark, moody, dangerous and - he takes the term *bad boy* to a whole different level.

No.

Stop looking at him like that, Neve.

I sigh and try standing up. But I stumble and fall hard onto my ass again.

Dalila laughs and flops onto her side.

"Don't laugh at me. You try stand up." I giggle.

"I can stand up." She says boldly. "I have no legs." Her laughter slurs her words into a mumble.

The two men are staring at us as though we've lost our minds.

Dalila rolls onto her stomach again and pulls her legs beneath herself and braces her body by leaning onto her hands. It doesn't work.

And we are rolling with laughter again.

"We have to get them into bed." Mas says, unamused.

"You grab Dalila. I'll grab the bride." Celso says, stepping towards me. Mas looks like he wants to argue, but he presses his lips together and leans down to scoop his sister off the floor. "Really, Dalila?" He huffs. "What's Nevio going to say when he finds out you're this drunk?"

"*Really, Dalila.*" She mocks him, pulling a face. "I already *told* Nevio I'm on *best friend duty* for like the entire night." She sasses him. "Oh, my goodness I need to pee."

"For fuck sakes." Mas groans.

When Celso leans down and wraps his arms around my body, lifting me as though I weigh nothing at all and holding me cradled in his arms - I swoon.

Embarrassingly, I freaking swoon.

To make things worse - I rest my head on his shoulder and take a deep breath of his cologne. Oh. My. Goodness. He's sexy. He leans his head into me, and his lips brush over my neck. It sends goosebumps washing over my skin. My entire body lights with need.

He carries me through to the main bedroom and carefully lays me down on the bed. I take his hand and squint at him, grinning, probably looking like a complete maniac.

"You're kind of hot." I giggle. The smile that spreads across his lips is tainted with darkness.

"*Neve.*" Dalila says in horror.

"Sorry." I laugh louder, releasing Celso's hand.

She rolls across the bed from where Mas dumped her unceremoniously next to me and punches me in the arm.

"You may not date my brother." She says sternly, throwing me a dramatic, serious stare.

I giggle again and close my eyes. The entire room is spinning.

"Dalila—" I whisper.

"Mm—"

"Thank you." I mumble.

"I'd do anything for you, babe. You mean the world to me." She says, drunkenly draping her arm over me and snuggling herself into the pillow.

She's asleep and snoring when Celso comes back into the room carrying water and tablets.

"Sit up." He demands, his voice so captivating that I do exactly as I'm told. Dalila's arm flops off me, but she carries on snoring.

"Take this, or you're going to feel like death in the morning." He hands me water and gestures for me to open my mouth.

Narrowing my eyes at him for a second, I contemplate my life choices - my lips part.

He gently pushes two painkillers into my mouth, letting his fingers brush slowly across my lips.

A low growl rumbles through him.

Behind him Mas walks into the room.

"Let's go." He snaps. "We'll come check on them tomorrow."

Celso says nothing, but his eyes are like dreamy dark pools that are drawing me in.

That's the last thing I remember before I pass out next to my best friend on what was supposed to be my wedding day.

CHAPTER FOUR
Celso

Mas and I walk out of the hotel together. He is muttering about what a shit show this entire thing was.

"Someone doesn't just disappear." He says to me, his eyes narrowed.

"Yeah, it's crazy." I say, not thinking about the day or what happened because I'm thinking about Neve, lying upstairs asleep on that bed. Not married. Single. *Waiting for me.*

I'm thinking about the look she gave me tonight, and how she would have been putty in my hands if we had been alone.

"Yeah. Crazy." Mas mutters, tired and agitated. I can tell he wants to get into this conversation more - but he's not in the mood after such a long day. I'll hear about his concerns in the morning again. But he can talk till he's blue in the face. I've covered my tracks.

"Night." I wave at him as he climbs into his car. "Night." He sighs, closing the door and starting the engine.

I walk over to where I'm parked and climb into my car. Except I don't drive off. And once he's out of sight, his engine growling off into the distance, I climb out of my car and walk back into the hotel.

I can't get Neve out of my head and tonight is too good an opportunity to miss.

I have no idea how tomorrow is going to pan out, so I want to make the most of the current situation.

Dipping my hand into my pocket I find the penthouse keycard I stole off the entrance table of their room. My lips curve into a menacing grin as I stare at my reflection in the perfectly polished steel walls of the elevator. Straightening the black collar of my crisp shirt I dust my hands over my chest and roll the sleeves up over my forearms. By the time I'm done the elevator has stopped on the top floor.

It wouldn't even be odd for me to be coming back up here. I can say I forgot to take my phone, or I accidentally took the room key and wanted to return it.

I swipe the card and the door clicks, a little green light shows it is no longer locked.

Pushing it open, I quietly pull it closed behind myself.

The room isn't pitch dark. Lights from the chandelier in the living room are still on, turned really low and giving the place a warm yellow glow.

I set my phone down on the coffee table, next to the keycard and my car keys.

Quietly I make my way to the bedroom.

Dalila has rolled almost off the bed on her side. She is fast asleep with her face practically hanging off the edge, still snoring softly.

Neve has kicked her blankets half off and her wedding dress has shifted up, showing off her long shapely legs. She's lying on her back with one leg bent upward as though she was dancing in her sleep.

I reach out and run my hand from her ankle, slowly, over her smooth skin, perfectly silky, warm, and inviting, up over her thigh. I pause with my fingers resting on her inner thigh.

My cock is throbbing so hard it hurts, pressed against the seams of my pants.

I glance across the bed and pull my lips tight.

Fuck.

"If only we were alone, I'd finally show you how special you are to me." I whisper, letting my fingers drift higher, beneath the wedding dress.

Neve stirs and I freeze for a moment, my heart beating fast, adrenaline pumping wildly inside me. I love it. The thrill of it.

The challenge.

There is no fear, only excitement.

She mumbles something and rolls onto her side with her legs curled up towards her chest.

Her long blonde hair is spilled across the pillow in a mess of half braided curls and twists.

I gently brush my fingers through it, untangling one of the braids.

"If you were mine, I would have taken proper care of you before you fell asleep." I whisper. "I would have helped you into something more comfortable. Brushed your hair and given you something to eat."

I sit on the edge of the bed in the curve of her petite body.

For half an hour I run my fingers through her hair, untangling and brushing out the knots. Her hair is now spread out behind her like a silky wave.

Dalila stirs and sighs loudly.

Shit.

She rolls over to face me and for a moment I think her eyes are open. But they aren't.

I should go.

I've been here too long as it is.

Leaning over Neve with my hand resting on the bed above her head, I softly press my mouth over her lips and taste her sweetness.

She moves her head away, frowning in her sleep.

"Good night, my angel." I whisper, stepping back, reluctant to go - but everything is set in motion now and it won't be long before it all falls into place.

She is mine.

She will soon realize it wasn't a choice I was giving her. I was predicting the future when I told her she belongs to me.

On the drive home I have nothing but excitement for what is waiting for me. In a way, I'm glad we weren't alone tonight. Perhaps our first time should be more planned out. Something special, intimate. Not that I think there is anything more beautiful than fucking her in a wedding dress.

I would prefer it to be the wedding dress she wears for me.

The more I think about her the more my body fills with desire. It's always like this when I see her. When I'm near her, I lose control of my thoughts.

But I am reassured that this is one of the last times I will have to handle the situation myself, alone, without her touch and without her silky-smooth skin.

After a hot shower I climb into bed satisfied, for the moment. I am a patient man, but it was wearing thin regarding Neve. I don't want to wait anymore.

From here on out I'm going to be more aggressive in my pursuit of her. It's time.

I fall asleep thinking about our future. And picturing how beautiful she looked with my hand on her skin.

Bright, warm sunshine splashes onto my pillow and pulls me from the dream I was lost in.

My dreams are never pleasant. Always dark and filled with shadowed mysteries that want to tear me apart. I sneer, pressing my hands against my eyes to push the last remnants of those haunting images from my mind. In the real world I do whatever the fuck I want. I take what I want, and I am whoever I want to be. No one can touch me. No one can control me.

But in my dreams, I'm always running. Always drowning. Always terrified.

Sighing loudly, I toss the heavy blankets away from my body and swing my legs over the edge of the bed.

Soft, thick carpet beneath my toes reminds me I'm in the real world. Everything is okay.

Ever since I was young sleeping has been an issue for me. The day I found out my mother left, discarding me as though I was some unwanted burden.

My father has always treated me differently. Not bad. Not bad at all. He has favored me, protected me, solved every single one of my problems. He's supported my choices and never punished me - not like he did to my older brothers.

I know it's not only because I am the youngest. I think it has more to do with my mother than me.

He had an affair, cheating on his wife, Francesca - the mother of all of my siblings - with *my* mother, Amelia.

I think the memory of Amelia is what draws him to me. It's the reason he treats me with unfair preference. I never met her because she disappeared only a few months after I was born and left my father to raise me on his own. Of course, when I say on his own, I mean with the help of a team of housekeepers and nursemaids.

But I never met my mother. Her being so willing to walk away from me without ever glancing back - that changed my view of women.

But Neve is different.

And I want her.

And I will make sure that I get her.

The coffee is dark and sweet, and it filters away the last of my nightmares.

Sunday mornings are the quietest mornings of my week. My phone doesn't ring, and no one is asking anything of me. It's also the loneliest mornings of my week.

My penthouse in the city overlooks the vast expanse of buildings, networks of streets filled with ant-like people far below, hurrying from one place to another. I can see people, I can hear the cars and the life around me - but I am alone.

I've always felt this sense of departure from my brothers and sister. They live in a different world from me - a world un-abandoned - a world in which they have found love.

It's all I want at the end of the day. That unconditional love.

From Neve.

My phone rings and I narrow my eyes in annoyance. Who is calling me? What do they want?

For fuck sakes. I am not in the mood to deal with Mas right now.

"I'm downstairs, open up." He demands as soon as I answer the call.

My jaw clenches. He acts like he owns everyone.

Pressing the keypad near the front door I snap back. "It's open."

He hangs up and I return to staring out across the views from my balcony.

I could push Mas over the side and say it was an accident. I chuckle.

Perhaps I'll save that for another day.

Mas walks into my penthouse like he owns the place, dumping his keys on the entrance table and walking straight into the kitchen to make himself a coffee.

"Morning." I say sarcastically.

"We need to talk." He replies coldly, using his *I'm the oldest, and that automatically puts me in charge of everything* voice.

"What about?" I ask, leaning one elbow against the kitchen counter and sipping the last of my coffee.

"You know exactly what we need to talk about. Don't play dumb with me. Where is the guy?" he hisses.

I smirk. "Why in the world would I do anything to that worthless idiot?"

"Because you want his fiancé, and he was in your way. We know how you deal with people who get in your way, Celso - but this guy is the son of a very wealthy and powerful businessman. It's too public. It's too risky. Whatever you did—"

"I didn't do anything man, calm the fuck down." I roll my eyes dramatically.

Mas stands in *my* kitchen looking at me as though I've done something wrong and he's about to send me to the naughty corner.

Agitation flares through me.

"Listen. You need to get the fuck over this idea of yours. I didn't touch the asshole. He stood her up. He doesn't deserve her. End of story."

Mas continues to stare at me.

"Dammit, Celso." He mutters under his breath. It's clear he doesn't believe me, but he has nothing to go on. Besides, what the hell is he going to do? Nothing.

There's nothing he could do even if I had a giant sign on my face saying, "I did it."

Mas doesn't have much else to say to me, so when his coffee is finished, he leaves, and I'm left on my own again. Thinking about Neve and our future.

CHAPTER FIVE
Neve

I hear a loud, pain filled groan before I open my eyes. At first, I'm not sure if it was me that made the noise or not, but as I slowly get dragged into the devastating reality of my hangover - Dalila groans again.

"What the hell." I mumble, rolling over and an intense, heavy headache throbs behind my eyes. "How much did we drink?"

"All of it." Is her only answer, and it makes me chuckle. But laughing hurts even more so I put a stop to that.

"I think I might puke." Her voice is tight.

"As long as it isn't anywhere where I'd have to clean it up - "

She sits up and looks over at me, her hair a tangled mess, knotted in yesterday's braids. I reach up and touch my own, already worried about how much of a challenge it's going to be to get these braids out - but my hair is silky soft and falling over my shoulders in neat waves.

There isn't a single braid in my hair and all the pins and clips are set on the bedside table.

"What the fuck?" I mumble. There is no way I did that last night. I couldn't even string a sentence together - never mind worrying about brushing my hair.

"Did you take my braids out?" I ask.

She lifts one corner of her lip and squints one of her eyes. "Are you kidding me?" she says.

I can't for the life of me figure it out, but there are more immediate things that need my attention right now. Like painkillers. Coffee. Water. More pain killers. And please, for the love of all things that are good and wonderful on this green Earth - I need to get out of this wedding dress. It's cutting into me in the most uncomfortable ways and the skirt is completely twisted around my legs. I have no idea how I slept throughout the night wearing it - well I guess I know - I was freakishly drunk.

I stand up, hating how it feels, clutching onto one of the four-bed pillars.

The world spins a little and I swallow back a nauseous wave.

"Coffee." She says.

"Coffee." I agree.

Thank goodness they have one of those one-push-button machines that does it all for you.

I really hope my stomach can handle this coffee because my brain desperately needs it.

"Here." Dalila says, handing me a couple of painkillers.

"Thanks." I murmur.

"Are you doing, ok?" She asks, and I know she isn't referring to the hangover.

I sigh softly and bite at my lower lip. "I don't know. I think I need to first get over this waking up thing - I can assess how I am emotionally after that." I say, not having the mental or physical capacity to unpack that disaster and all its intricacies.

We sit quietly drinking coffee and waiting for the headaches to stop drumming entire songs inside our skulls. Dalila scrapes herself off the chair and sighs. "I better get going. Nevio is asking where I am and if I don't start moving now, I'm going to climb back into that bed and stay there all day."

"Same. I'm going to hop into the shower and get out of this damned dress. Before you go, will you help me untie the corset thingy?"

She giggles. "Where would you be without me?"

Checking my phone was a mistake.

It's not like I expected anything other than what it is - but now I have anxiety on top of everything else.

My face is on every possible news site, plastered all over social media and most likely on every newspaper throughout the city.

They have a picture of me, standing alone at the

doors that lead into the church, holding those flowers and looking utterly lost.

What made him decide not to marry her?

Where is the groom?

Runaway groom leaves stricken bride at the altar.

Embarrassing night for Neve Greco as her fiancé is a no show on their wedding.

The headlines are endless - and horrible.

Standing in the elevator with Dalila, heading down into the foyer with my little overnight bag on the floor next to me, the wedding dress rather brutally shoved into it along with the rest of my clothes from yesterday - I close my eyes and count to three.

Stop looking at your phone. Stop stressing about it. Get home. Deal with one thing at a time.

But, as soon as those elevator doors slide open I realize another big mistake I've made. I didn't ask the hotel staff to escort me out of the back entrance.

The foyer is flooded with reporters and cameras fire off bright flashes of light.

"Oh, my word." Dalila squeals in horror.

"Walk - keep your head down." I say to her, speaking loud enough to be heard over one hundred questions being blasted at me.

"Why did he decide not to marry you, Neve?"

"Were you two having problems?"

"Can you tell us if one of you was having an affair?"

"How did it feel to be stood up at the alter?"

I want to punch them in the face. Their questions are heartless and cruel. They don't give a shit about what I went through - they only care about the headlines. The best story. And this, right now, is the best story.

We tackle our way out of the foyer with the help of the hotel staff who finally realize what is going on and come to our rescue. "You can't be in here." One of them shouts angrily to a cameraman.

"Where did you park?" Dalila asks.

"Right here." I say, pointing to my car.

Last night they were supposed to take it away and send it back home for me - I was supposed to leave this morning in a limousine, headed for the airport.

But obviously someone made the right choice and left it here for me. Thank goodness.

I climb in and Dalila waves goodbye, and hurries towards her own car.

In the silence of my car, driving through the city towards my apartment - my heart is heavy. I'm grateful that the painkillers seem to work, dulling it to a mild thirty percent of the pain than what it was before, but now with the headache gone my mind is free to think about everything else.

"Where are you, Damion?" I ask no one as I turn into the underground parking of my building.

The security is ridiculously strict, so I am not worried about reporters here. But I am worried about how I'm supposed to deal with all of this.

What am I supposed to do now?

Hurrying up to my apartment a wave of relief washes over me as I step inside and pull the door shut behind myself. I remember what I told Dalila last night. I told her I was relieved when I didn't have to marry Damion and it's true. I am still relieved now - but that doesn't mean that I wanted anything bad to happen to him and I have no doubt that something has happened.

Damion is not the type of person who would stand me up. And I think he was pretty excited to marry me.

I push the suitcase up against the wall next to the front door, knowing it will sit there for a few days before I deal with it. A tinge of guilt pokes at me because the dress is in there.

Dammit.

Fine.

Unzipping the top, I yank the dress out but leave everything else.

I shake it out and toss it over the back of one of my dining room chairs.

Flopping onto my sofa I slide my phone open to check my messages.

So many friends have sent me their condolences - but I flip past those. I'm looking for clues, hints, trails, anything that might tell me what happened to Damion.

When my phone dies, I plug it in and grab my Mac Air, sitting with my legs curled beneath me I go through his social media, his friends' pages, his emails which are still open on my Mac from the last time he logged in to check them. Nothing is out of the ordinary. Nothing is weird or alarming or suspicious. He up and vanished into thin air.

"Oh shit." I say excitedly. "I have keys to his apartment."

In a split second, my mind is made up. I have to go there. I'm convinced his parents, or his brother would have already checked it out, but I want to see for myself. There might be something they overlooked.

He lives only two streets away from me and there is a coffee shop in between us, so I decide to walk and stop for a takeaway on the way. Maybe something to eat as well because my stomach is settling.

The first few minutes of the walk aren't too bad, but of course, I underestimate the determination of reporters - and now they are following me.

Running is the last thing I want to do today, but I have no choice as I move faster and faster towards the coffee shop which is now some kind of sanctuary ahead of me - I need to get off the streets.

Bursting through the doors, breathless and mildly panicked, everyone inside turns to glare at me in shock.

Reporters flock outside the doors. I don't make eye contact.

Instead, I head over to a table in the corner, sit down and pull out my phone so that I have something to do with my hands and somewhere to look.

My cheeks are glowing red.

I hate this.

I hate everything about this.

A sweet server comes over and greets me by my name, showing that she recognizes me from one article.

"Hi, Neve, what can I get you today?"

I pull my mouth tight.

"Coffee - and uh - a toasted cheese with bacon and that pesto-type sauce you guys usually have."

"I won't be long." She smiles, and I breathe a sigh of relief. No questions. No nosy poking into my business.

Because I have nothing else to do but wait - I start messaging people. Anyone I can think of. His friends, my friends, his work colleagues. Someone knows *something*.

And by the time my toasted sandwich arrives I have discovered that the night before our wedding Damion went out for a drink with a friend of his - they left the bar at the same time and that seems to be the last time he was seen.

After that no one heard a single thing. Not a message, not a phone call, not a whisper.

Maybe I should get a private investigator. The police will poke around, but apart from a distraught bride who got abandoned on her wedding day, there is no evidence of foul play - *yet*. His family is influential though. They will pull some strings.

I'll have to call his mom later and find out what they are doing.

In the meantime, I want to talk to my father and see if he'll help me.

Something about this is wrong.

I have a horrible feeling that something bad has happened to him.

CHAPTER SIX
Celso

I kick my feet up, resting them on the coffee table. My father usually complains at my brothers when they do this, but he always pretends he doesn't notice when I do it.

The twins are playing cards to pass the time on a lazy afternoon while we wait for dinner to be ready.

My father made a new rule after everyone started getting married and disappearing from his life - he decided that every second Wednesday we had to be at his place for dinner. All of us. No spouses, only his kids. If you ask me, it's a slap in the face to tell your partner they can't come to a family dinner. I would never do that to Neve.

My brothers are assholes for leaving their wives home alone.

Masaccio tilts his chin towards me, gesturing at the newspaper lying on the coffee table.

"No sign of the fiancé yet." He says.

My father, sitting next to me on the sofa reading a different newspaper, grunts in response.

Masaccio is like a hound with the scent of blood. He stands up and walks over to us, sitting down opposite my father.

"Dad, I have concerns about this guy's disappearance. Concerns that will affect the whole family."

"What are you talking about?" My father says in a huff, dropping his own newspaper in a scrunch on his lap so that he can glare at Masaccio.

Tuomo is riveted by the conversation. Rufino and Dalila are in the kitchen getting drinks.

Masaccio lowers his voice emphasizing the seriousness of this conversation.

"Dad, if Celso did something to this guy it will cause a massive backfire for our family. His actions are reckless and selfish and—"

The look in my father's eyes is terrifying. Glaring straight at Masaccio he snarls, "If you utter one more word of this, I swear you will be the one bearing the consequences - from me. Never speak ill of your own brother like that. We are family. Cosa Nostra. Don't forget where you come from, Masaccio. We don't throw each other under the fucking bus."

I smirk and it seems to edge Masaccio towards losing control.

His fists clench in anger.

"Dad, Celso did something to this guy—"

My father stands up and grabs Masaccio around the collar of his shirt. Mas is bigger than him. In a fight my father wouldn't stand a chance. But this is a different power.

"Leave your brother alone." He growls darkly, so close to Masaccio that Mas is leaning his head back to get away.

My father releases my brother and sits down again.

Mas is fuming, but he pulls himself together and dusts his hands over his shirt and sits down again.

His mouth is so tight the muscles along his jaw are flexed and rigid.

He won't look at me.

He won't look at my father.

I can't hide the grin on my face. His discomfort is pleasing to me. I lean forward to pick up the newspaper from the table, but my chest tightens when I see my sister's face - Dalila is standing in the doorway, her head tilted to the side and her mouth hanging open. She's frozen in horror and staring straight at me. I would have preferred for her not to overhear that conversation.

"Celso?" She asks, timidly. "Did you - did you do something to Damion?"

"Who?" I ask, playing it down.

"Neve's fiancé. Damion." She says more boldly, walking towards me, fierce confrontation in her eyes. She stands in front of the sofa and glares at me.

"Leave your brother alone. All of you." My father says. He waves his hand in the air to dismiss the tense atmosphere.

The chef comes through to announce that dinner is ready.

"Oh great. I'm starving." I smile, standing up.

Mas and Dalila stare at each other in disbelief - but they know better than to push their luck once my father has spoken.

Dinner might've been awkward if I'd paid any attention to their constant glares. Their eyes boring into me like accusations. But I didn't.

My father always has my back, even when he's angry with me I never feel it, I just sense mild disappointment, and we move on.

We sit eating quietly, the sound of forks and knives clinking against plates is the only thing I hear. Red is playing on his phone which is usually frowned at during dinner, but I think my father has given up dealing with everyone today.

Mas, Dalila, and I are locking in this weird silent thing.

Tuomo is ignoring the entire shit show.

I stab my fork into a piece of pink steak and shove it into my mouth.

Masaccio being angry at me is unjustified. He doesn't know the whole story. Neve should never have gotten engaged to that guy in the first place. She is *mine*. She has belonged to me for a while now and I made that truly clear to her.

Her father wouldn't even be where he is today if it wasn't for my family.

Dinner drags on in boring silence until the housekeeper clears dishes and I stand up, ready to leave.

"Thanks for dinner, dad. I'm going to head out now."

"Alright Kiddo. I'll walk you out." He says, standing up and following me out of the dining room. He slips his arm around my shoulders and whispers to me, leaning close. "Keep your head down, kiddo."

"I will, dad, don't worry." I smile and give him a one-armed hug. "I'll see you soon."

He waits on the top step until I reach my car. Mas and Dalila are busy saying goodbye to him while I'm tossing my jacket onto the back seat before I climb in.

"Celso." Mas calls my name as I'm about to duck into the car.

"What?" I snap. I'm over his pestering.

"Hold up a second." He says, Dalila following him as my father waves one last time, steps back into the house and closes the front door on us.

Mas walks straight towards me, grabs the front of my shirt, and slams my back against the car.

"Where the fuck is he?" he snarls into my face.

I glance towards the front door.

"Don't look for daddy - fight your own fucking battles." Mas growls at me.

Anger shoots through me like an arrow. My heart beating loud in my ears, blood pumping through my head and making the veins on my temple throb.

"Get the fuck off me." I shove him backwards, and when he comes running back towards me, I swing, and my fist connects with his jaw.

"You want to fight me?" He shouts, wrapping his hand around my throat and slamming his fist into my left cheek.

I kick him hard and he loses his footing and falls onto his knees. Throwing myself at him we both end up tumbling onto the ground with dirt kicking up around us as we roll and fight.

"Stop." Dalila shouts in a panic.

I ignore her as I carry on trying to hit my brother.

I'm tired of him thinking he's better than me. He's not.

We wrestle until Rufino and Tuomo pull us apart. Rufino shoves me into my car and tells me to get the fuck out of here before he gets involved in the fight too. He glares at me, the thick scar across his face is a reminder of what he's capable of.

Rufino is a brute of a man and not someone you want to mess with. By sheer size alone I have respect for him - never mind being aware of the reason they call him the Red Dragon. He's not someone you want to be on the wrong side of.

He slams my door shut, and I start the engine, not bothering to glance towards Masaccio, who is still going on about how I've done something and everyone else is ignoring it.

"He's guilty. It's fucking obvious!" He shouts.

I rev the engine to drown him out, and wheel spin, kicking gravel up from behind my car as I pull out into the road and away from those idiots.

I'm too tense to go home so I go to the only place where I will find some peace.

Neve's apartment building.

It's late and she'll be home. I want to see her for a bit, watch her, reassure myself that our time is coming - sooner than she thinks.

The media has been savage with covering her story. They've accused her of cheating and driving him away. They've accused him of cheating and running away with the new love of his life. They've made up a whirlwind of stories to keep readers entertained.

Of course, some of those stories involve Damion being murdered and them looking for a body. It's all speculation at this point. No one knows anything for sure, and without evidence it will stay that way.

I park in my usual spot, away from the entrance of her apartment building because the security cameras are pretty tight around the building.

Opening the glove compartment, I pull out my binoculars and turn my attention onto her windows.

Neve always has her curtains open into her living room area. I can see the entire space and the kitchen, which is open plan, connected to the living room. She doesn't seem to have any concept of privacy.

Neve walks into the kitchen, she's talking to someone. Her face scrunched, her little nose wrinkled up as she discusses something distasteful. I move the binoculars, searching for the other person and my chest tightens horribly when I see a man follow her into the kitchen. Who the fuck is this?

"What the fuck does she think she's doing?" I snarl loudly.

Focusing on the guy my heart clenches. He looks like Damion. For a second, I think it might even be him, but obviously that's impossible.

Logic overrides the panic bolting through my body.

"It's his *brother*." I sigh in agitation. "What - does

he think he can slide in now, take what belongs to me? Make a move on my girl?"

Dropping the binoculars I take a deep breath. I have to calm down. Neve knows better. She wouldn't be interested in the brother, anyway. She was hardly interested in Damion, and I've freed her from that commitment - she won't be stupid enough to get locked into another one at this point.

And that asshole does not understand who he's messing with if he thinks he has a free shot at Neve now.

Coming to watch her was supposed to calm me down, but it's made me feel worse.

It would be best to go home and get some sleep, but I can't bring myself to drive away and leave - knowing there is a man in Neve's apartment with her.

So, I live with the fact that I have to stay until he leaves. For my peace of mind.

I keep watching them. They have a drink and talk - nothing appears to be going on between them. Finally, a hair before midnight, he hugs her tightly, holding her for longer than I am happy with, and then he leaves.

I stay longer, watching Neve clear away the glasses and wipe the kitchen counter.

I watch until that asshole's car pulls away from the building and he is one hundred percent gone. I stay another thirty minutes to make sure it's not some trick, and he will not come right back.

I won't allow another person to come between us.

It's my chance now.

I've worked hard to make this possible.

Nothing and no one is going to stop me.

CHAPTER SEVEN
Neve

"I need to get out, but we have to figure out a way so that the reporters don't follow me." I huff.

Dalila's voice carries through the phone. "Are they *still* at it? It's been almost two weeks."

"They'll be at it until people are bored with the story or until we finally figure out where he is."

"I hear you. They really are vultures. Ok - let me make a plan and arrange for a driver for us. I can come fetch you underground in a car they don't recognize, and we can go for a drink?"

"That sounds like exactly what I need. I'll go crazy

if I have to stare at the walls of my apartment for one more day. I want to feel normal for a second."

"Be ready at eight. I'll confirm details later." She says, and we say goodbye and hang up.

I breathe a sigh of relief. She has no idea how much I appreciate her.

Last night I invited Denver over. Damion's brother.

Denver is a splitting image of my brother, Luke. Not physically, but in personality.

He's stiff, uptight, poised and groomed to perfection.

His father has been grooming him since he was young to take over his business when the time comes, like my brother has been groomed to take over my father's political career, and I think his entire personality has become enveloped around his father's expectations of him. Denver and Luke could be twins in that regard.

I wanted to be subtle about questioning him - not to cause alarm for his family. But I still can't shake the idea that there was foul play somewhere along the line. I wanted to find out if Damion was involved in something he shouldn't have been.

Denver and him aren't very close though and he couldn't tell me much. His answers were very politically correct and cautious. It's how it's always been - every conversation I've ever had with Denver has been stiff.

It makes him a difficult person to communicate with and to be honest I was relieved when he left.

And also, no closer to finding out what has happened to Damion.

It seems his own family is trying to keep the entire fiasco as quiet as possible because the media coverage is not helping his dad's campaign. I reckon if it was boosting his numbers, he would be more interested in solving it. It's pretty disgusting if you ask me - to be so dismissive of your son's disappearance.

Last night Denver told me that Damion once disappeared for two months, right before starting college. He fell off the map and didn't have any contact with his family. He went on some sabbatical telling no one - climbed Machu Picchu and took ayahuasca in the desert somewhere. He wanted to 'find himself.'

I'm not convinced though. Even though getting married is a big thing that will change your life drastically, I still don't think Damion would do that to me.

As promised, Dalila messages me to let me know she will be downstairs at eight to steal me away for our night out. I can't wait. I get ready at six because I'm so excited to get out.

By eight I'm standing inside the door of the underground parking lot, partially hiding myself in case there are any reporters around, until Dalila's driver pulls up, and she pushes the back door open, grinning at me.

"Hey, you need a ride?" She laughs.

"Oh, my word - yes." I exclaim, hurrying into the car.

"Wow, you look incredible." She says, reaching out and touching my little black sequin dress. It's a little short, but I love it. It glitters when I move and makes me feel gorgeous.

"You don't look so bad yourself." I eye her up and down with a smirk. Her pale silver dress is going to get her a lot more attention that I think her husband would be pleased about. "Nevio is going to have competition tonight."

"Not a chance." She shakes her head. "Besides, I asked him to meet us there when he's done with the work he has to get through."

Stepping into the nightclub is like stepping into another world. Music pulses over my body, setting goosebumps flickering over my skin. Thick bass beats in my chest, vibrating against my rib cage.

I grin. This is exactly what I needed to clear my head. I've been so consumed by worries - I need to let it all go for one night so that I can think more clearly tomorrow.

People don't function very well when they're stressed.

"Let's get some shots." Dalila says, tugging me towards the bar.

She leans over and shouts something I can't hear to the bartender, and I stand next to her, already dancing a little and fully prepared to let my hair down tonight.

A few minutes later she hands me a tequila. "Oh dear." I grin.

"For tonight - you are *relaxing* - ok?" She says sternly.

"Agreed." I nod.

We clink the glasses together and I throw my head back, letting the tequila burn like fire down my throat.

I shudder and squint against the unpleasant taste, then bite down on a piece of pineapple splashed with tabasco. It's the only way I will ever have tequila.

Dalila nods, and grabs my hand, pulling me towards the dance floor. I don't argue one bit. I came here to dance. This is how I relax. I need this more than anything.

As predicted - guys are all over Dalila. She keeps having to glare at them or blatantly push them away from her while she's dancing. Once or twice, someone tries to make a move on me, but mostly I am free to dance and enjoy myself.

When we take a break and head to the bar for another drink, I laugh at her. "You attract a lot of attention." I tease.

"Oh, speak for yourself." She laughs.

"Whatever, you have guys falling over you."

"Did you not notice the row of guys trying to dance behind you?" She says, her brows knotted.

"Not really." I shrug.

"What does a guy have to do to get the attention of a gorgeous girl like this?" Mr. Tall Dark and Handsome slides up behind Dalila and wraps his hands around her waist. She grins, recognizing her husband's voice immediately.

"You came." She says excitedly, turning to kiss Nevio.

"Can I get you two a drink?" He asks, grinning at me. "How are you, Neve?"

I shrug. "As good as I can be at the moment, I guess."

"We aren't allowed to talk about bad things tonight." Dalila waves her hand at her husband, letting him know the rules. "We're here to have fun." She raises her brows, and he holds up both hands in defense. "Fun it is then." He chuckles.

After another round of tequila, Nevio leads us to the VIP table he arranged and the two of them sit down to catch up a little.

"I'm going to dance for a bit." I shout over the music.

"I'll be there soon." Dalila grins.

"No rush, enjoy yourself." I smile and turn away, making my way to the dance floor alone. I want to get lost in the music again. I want to dance until my feet ache and I'm so tired that I have no problems falling asleep tonight.

I've been dancing for about half an hour when hands run up over my waist. I turn, expecting to see Dalila wiggling through the dance floor to come and join me, but I find myself face to face with Celso.

My heart stops beating for a second and my lips drop open.

"What are you doing here?" I stammer.

He smirks, his lips curving up at the corners, creating dimples on his cheeks. His bright blue eyes are catching the lights and the look he's giving me is making me think some very inappropriate thoughts.

I try to step away from him, but the dance floor is too crowded, and I bump into the guy behind me. Celso grabs me around the waist and pulls me tight up against his chest.

The way he handles me it's so forceful, so deliberate. It really turns me on. Until I met him, I never knew I would be attracted to a man who takes control.

Damion was always a little too polite. Slightly disinterested. It was almost a duty for him to be romantic with me and I really felt it.

With Celso, the way he hunts me down - it's so primal. Like the look he's giving me now.

"This dress—" he growls. "Did you wear it for me?"

"I - I didn't know you were coming." It's a stupid answer. The answer should be no, but I'm mesmerized by him and the tequila isn't helping me think straight.

His hand runs up my back, running over my spine and sending a heat wave through me that settles between my legs like a pulsing, urgent need.

I swallow hard.

Fuck. I need to create some distance between us before I do something stupid.

Celso is not the guy you get involved with.

I bite my lip and try turn my head away from him, but he moves boldly, wrapping his hand around my jaw, his long fingers digging into my cheeks.

Celso leans forward and presses his mouth over mine.

For a moment I can't breathe. I am consumed by the kiss. I don't even try to fight it or deny him.

My entire body is on fire.

But my logic snaps back into place and I manage to push him away from me.

"What the fuck?" I snap angrily, wiggling from his grasp and turning my back on him.

I don't wait for his response, instead I storm off to the bar to get another tequila to numb away this heightened sensation of desire flooding me.

The *last thing I need right now* is the media getting a photo of me kissing some mafia goon only a week after my wedding fell apart.

"Tequila." I snap at the bartender, then feel bad for being rude. I throw him an apologetic smile. He doesn't seem to notice my attitude or my apology.

Celso slides into place next to me, leaning against the bar as though he owns this city.

"What do you want, Celso?" I demand, agitated by his presence and the things it's doing to my body.

"I want you, Neve. And it's about time you admitted that we should be together."

"Be together?" I ask, exasperated by his confidence.

"I know you've been hanging out with other guys and I'm warning you to watch your step, my angel. You belong to me. Don't forget that."

I narrow my eyes at him as my desire turns into thick anger at his audacity.

"I *belong* to you?" I snap. "Belong?"

What the fuck is wrong with this asshole?

"Neve." He says, with warning his tone that turns me on even more. Even my anger isn't enough to quench that need.

"Celso." I hiss back, rich with sarcasm.

His eyes grow darker than I've ever seen them before.

He steps closer and talks down to me. "You are mine. The sooner you accept that the easier it will be for you. Don't push me, angel."

I shove him hard, my hand pressed against his muscular chest, he hardly moves but I've made my point because he takes one step away from me.

I burst out laughing.

His arrogance needs to be checked.

"You think that you and I would ever be a thing? You - some mafia criminal with no future and no proper place in society. Girls like me don't date guys like you. We date status, money, and class." I blurt out my words in an angry string of insults.

His lips curl, his jaw muscles feathering. The five o'clock shadow of dark stubble only makes him hotter.

Turning my face away, I shut my eyes to get my hormones under control.

Celso is livid, and he's not even trying to hide it.

CHAPTER EIGHT
Celso

Standing at the bar staring at Neve I have to clench my fists tightly to stop myself from grabbing her and dragging her lips up against mine again. Her attitude is nothing but a tease. A challenge I accept. I will wear her down. I will break her.

She will love me.

She's so fucking full of it - talking to me like that in public. Humiliating me in that way. If we were alone, I would have punished her for this.

She would have been begging me for mercy while I set sharp slaps across her ass cheeks. Maybe I'd have to tie her up. She looks like she might enjoy putting up a fight.

I snarl, biting down hard and fighting for control.

"Who the fuck do you think you're talking to, Neve?" I snarl at her.

"Oh, I'm not *your angel* anymore?" she sasses back at me, her hand on her hip as she puts it out to the side. Her lips are full and pink, and I want to kiss them again.

"You are *mine*." I hiss, reaching out and grabbing her jaw. Her lips are inches from mine and the taste of her mouth is still burning on my skin. My cock stirs as I stare into her bright blue eyes. She looks fierce, but she can't hide the fact that she wants me. Despite her words her body's response to my touch is glaringly obvious. She wouldn't say no.

"Celso?" Dalila's voice is tight with anger. "What are you doing?" Nevio is right behind her, his brows knotted at me as he stands braced for anything. Nevio is a dark character. I know he is capable of things that might surprise me. But he should not underestimate me either.

"Nothing." I say, dropping my hand down and stepping back. Neve rubs her hand over her face as though she is trying to rub the sensation of my touch off her skin.

"Neve, are you ok?" Dalila asks, looking towards her friend with concern.

"Of course I am, this asshole was just leaving." Neve looks me up and down with disgust.

"Actually, I just got here, and I have no intention of leaving." I smirk and it seems to agitate her further which amuses me.

"For fuck's sake, Celso." Dalila snaps, annoyed.

"It's ok, Dalila - I think I'm ready to head home, anyway." Neve sighs, turning away from the bar. I don't want her to go. I was hoping she would stay and dance with me.

"I'll give you a lift." Nevio says, stepping between Neve and myself. I glare at him. I wouldn't underestimate him - but I would take him down in a matter of seconds to get to Neve if I needed to. No one will ever come between us.

"Thanks." Neve mutters and Dalila reaches out to take her hand.

Nevio walks right behind them, blocking my view of both girls.

I hear Dalila's words as they walk away.

"Please be careful of Celso, remember your promise."

The warning sends thick rage pulsing through me. She's referring to the promise not to date any of her brothers. Even my sister is against me. But none of them will stop us from being together.

Standing alone at the bar I order three tequilas. Lining them up and shooting them back one after the other.

I order three more.

Neve's words are looping in my head. Tainting my thoughts and fueling the fire of anger inside me. *Girls like me don't date guys like you - mafia criminal with no future -*

I have more money and more power than any man she could ever be with. I can give her everything. The entire world. But she dares to humiliate me like that. She would be lucky to have a man like me. If she gave me half a chance, she would see that.

I keep drinking, knowing that her words were only her way of trying to deny the desire she has towards me. But that doesn't make me feel any better and soon the tequila is burning in my blood, and my anger is out of control.

I decide to dance to work off some of the frustration.

I make my way to the dance floor. Pushing people out of my way as I pass them, leaving them angry and muttering. What the fuck do I care.

Music throbs in the air around me, vibrating against my skin, blurring my thoughts. This is what I needed. The loud pulsing bass leaves no room in my mind for her words to continue looping. Sweat runs down my back beneath my shirt making it stick to me.

The heat of my emotions is fading when some fucking asshole shoves me from behind.

I spin around to face him, and he mutters something about watching where I move.

"What?" I snarl at him.

"I said watch yourself asshole." He spits, drunk and unsteady. His pale eyes are shifting as though he isn't ready for the challenge he's asked for.

"Watch myself?" I laugh.

Before he has a chance to say another word, I swing my fist and the snap of his nose as it shatters is the most satisfying sound I've heard all week.

He screams and with blood pouring down his face he fights back.

In no time at all the dance floor is cleared and it's the two of us battling it out in the open space. I'm sitting on his chest, my fists slamming into his face repeatedly. I hear people around me screaming and begging me to stop, but I can't. He crossed the wrong person today, and he's going to learn his lesson. Everyone should know not to fuck with me. *I own this city.*

Hands tug at me from behind, strong hands, pulling me off and dragging me from him. Three guys flock over him. He's not moving. His face is covered in blood, so is the floor.

The bouncers drag me out of the club and push me up against the wall.

"You fucking idiot, what the fuck was that? You might have killed him."

"The ambulance is on the way." Another one says.

"And the cops?"

"Yeah, they are almost here."

I try to push off the wall so that I can leave, but two of them pin me down again.

"Fucking get off me." I snap.

"You aren't going anywhere." The bouncer snarls.

I hold my hand in the air and grin. "Fine, but I need to make a phone call."

"Yeah, call your lawyer you arrogant fuck." One of them says sarcastically.

I don't call my lawyer. I call my father.

The cops arrive as I slide my phone back into my pocket. They park right outside the entrance, lights flashing as they climb out, arrogant and smug.

They come at me with aggression which I could challenge - but I allow them to handcuff me. And even when they slam me up against the side of their car I'm smirking.

"What the fuck is his problem?" one cop mutters to the other.

Patting me down he digs around in my pocket, pulling out whatever he finds.

"He won't stop smiling. Hey, fuck face, what are you smiling about? You're going to jail."

"He's probably high."

"Oh shit - I know who this is." His partner stammers, flipping my wallet open and looking at the name on my credit card.

Nervously he shifts and glances around himself. "Shit." He mutters. "Ah. Dude, no, we need to—"

"What are you doing to my son?" My father's voice makes them both spin around.

"Uh - he was in a fight." The nervous cop mutters. "Mr. Vece, we weren't aware—"

"Vincent Vece?" the other cop says in shock, finally catching up with the rest of us.

A deep chuckle rumbles through me while I enjoy their nervous discomfort.

"It's ok boys. You were doing your job." My father says calmly, handing them an envelope that no doubt has a thick wad of cash in it. "I understand the other guy started the fight?" he asks, his brows raised.

"Yeah, it was the other guy." They both nod, their bodies rigid and tense.

"Then why is my son in handcuffs?"

"Oh this - it was just - it was - *take them off.*" Cop number two hisses at his partner who fumbles with the key and releases me.

I turn to face them, snatching my wallet out of cop number one's hands. "Have a nice night *boys*." I smirk.

My father pulls his mouth tight and glares at me.

I grin. "Thanks, dad. It really was the other guy who started it."

"Go home, Celso. I told you to keep your head down."

I nod. "Yeah, I'm going home now. This place is a shit hole, anyway." My father watches as I walk towards my car and climb inside. When I drive off, he is still standing next to the cop car.

On my way I pass an ambulance, sirens blaring as it rushes towards the club with its emergency lights flashing and blinding me.

"So dramatic." I mutter, turning off the main street and heading towards my penthouse.

At home I'm pacing up and down. I can't stop thinking about what she said.

She didn't mean it.

She will soon find out for herself that I am the right man for her.

My sister needs to stop interfering. So does Masaccio. He needs to mind his own fucking business.

Or I need to find another way to get to Neve.

If Neve wants to play hard to get, I will play harder to get her.

That night, lying in bed, staring up at the stark white ceiling, my mind is churning with options and ideas. She doesn't stand a chance. I won't stop until I have her.

CHAPTER NINE
Neve

Nevio and Dalila drive me home, dropping me off underground right near the elevator.

"I'll walk you to your door." Nevio says, pushing his door open and getting ready to climb out.

"Don't be silly. This place is like a fortress. I'll be fine. Thank you, guys, so much for an awesome night out. I really enjoyed it." I smile.

"Sorry about my brother." Dalila sighs.

"It's ok, honestly. It's nothing to worry about." I brush it off, acting nonchalant. But the problem is that I am worried about it.

I'm worried about how fucking attracted I am to him.

He has this mannerism about him I can't ignore. He's magnetic. Demanding. Obsessive and possessive. I've never had a guy pursue me so intensely before and it's fucking incredibly hot.

"Message me when you get upstairs." Dalila says sternly.

"Yes, mom." I laugh, climbing out of the car.

"Hey." Dalila shouts through the window. "I'm serious."

"I know. I will. Bye guys." I wave before I step through the door and into the building.

The place is quiet. I climb into the elevator and for a moment I fantasize about Celso blocking the door before it closes all the way. I close my eyes and lean my head against the stainless-steel wall.

He pushes his way into the elevator and shoves me up against the wall, his hand locked around my throat. I cry out, my eyes wild with fright. His breath is hot against my mouth as he growls. "You will enjoy this, my angel." His other hand brushes up my body, dragging my dress higher as he leans into me, his cock hard against my stomach. His muscular, broad shoulders towering over me.

"Get off me, asshole." I mutter, feebly pushing him away. He grabs my wrists and pins them above my head.

He chuckles. "Don't lie to me, angel. Stop fighting this." His hand pushes between my legs and his finger dips inside me.

I gasp in fright when the elevator chimes, the doors sliding open on the top floor, right outside my door.

"What the fuck was that?" I mutter to myself, self-consciously tugging my dress down.

Once I'm safely in my apartment I message Dalila a picture of myself sticking my tongue at her while I stand in my kitchen, the kettle boiling behind me so I can make a cup of tea before I crawl into bed.

While I'm waiting, I tug my dress off and toss it over one of the bar chairs under the kitchen counter.

I already kicked my high heels off at the door so now I'm standing in only my underwear enjoying the cool night air against my skin.

I guess I should hop in the shower too. I'm a little sweaty from dancing.

An image of Celso pressed against my naked body flashes through my mind.

"Holy shit, girl. Get yourself under control."

I decide to shower before I make the tea because I'm hoping the cold water will clear these intense thoughts I'm having about my best friends brother. The one I promised her I wouldn't get involved with. The one I already *know* would be a bad idea to be involved with.

Climbing under the warm flow of water I sigh with pleasure.

I'd only get my heart broken. There is nothing good that can come from dating a fuckboy like him. He'd sleep with me - get bored - move on.

Although even a one-night stand with him would be fucking hot. And Dalila wouldn't need to find out.

No, Neve. Stop it.

I push the shower handle all the way to the cold side and squeal loudly when the temperature changes and icy water falls all over my body. But the shock of it clears my mind.

It's exactly what I need and when I head back into the kitchen with a big towel around me, dripping water from my feet and walking carefully so I don't slip - I feel better. More focused.

The tea bag swooshes around in my mug as I carry it to my room. I always leave the tea bag in because I prefer strong tea. Sweet and strong.

The towel drops to the floor, and I flick the covers back, wiggling my naked body beneath the sheets, pulling them up around my chin. The cold shower left me cold. Which I guess was the whole point of it.

My thoughts simmer down as I sit in my bed, cradling my tea mug in my hand and letting the ceramic warm my fingers.

Celso seems hell bent on winning me over. He's been telling me for years now that I belong to him and one day he'll make it happen.

I usually brush his comments off, ignoring them or make a joke about them - but lately it's becoming more intense and of course, I've been enjoying his obsession a little more.

It's stupid of me to play with fire like this, but I can't help it. He makes me feel a certain way that I'm quickly learning is how I *want to feel*. I want a guy to be that into me. Excited to be with me. Determined and forceful.

A thought strikes me.

Out of the blue.

It makes me gasp and freeze in horror.

How far would Celso go to make sure that I become his?

I never took his obsession seriously, but I should have. All this time maybe he wasn't joking.

What would he be willing to do to have me?

Make my fiancé disappear?

My throat tightens and I can't even swallow my tea.

I set the mug down and sit up higher in bed. No. I'm being crazy. Celso is my best friend's brother.

It's not like he isn't capable.

Murder?

I wouldn't put it past him.

No. This is not helping.

I need to sleep, not get all wild and crazy in my thoughts staying awake for hours unable to process them.

I huff and snuggle down into the bed, pulling the covers over my shoulders.

Go to sleep, Neve.

The constant beat of my phone's ringtone infiltrates my dreams. For a while it doesn't register as anything I need to pay attention to. But it won't stop.

I blink my eyes open and realize it wasn't a dream, it's my phone - and it's still ringing.

In a hurry I reach out to grab it, squinting to see the time. Five AM.

My father.

My father never calls me this early.

"Dad?" I mumble into the phone, my voice croaky with sleep.

"Honey, are you awake? His voice was strained and tight. It makes me nervous.

"I am now?" I clear my throat and sit up, rubbing my eyes while my heart races faster, nervous for whatever this call is about.

"Neve, they found Damion," he says, almost a whisper.

"That's great." I say excitedly. "Where was he - what did he say?"

"No, sorry - I mean - they found his body. What's left of it."

"What's left of it?" I mumble, not able to process. "What do you mean?"

"He's dead sweetheart. I'm sorry."

"No, he can't be—"

"You need to be at the house at ten. We have a reporter coming over and we are going to give a controlled statement. Don't say a word to anyone about it. We don't need more rumors starting and the media getting out of control again."

He's still talking but I'm not taking any of it in. I'm in shock. Numb and cold and shaking.

Looking down at my hands I try my best to force my eyes to focus so that my mind can focus too.

But he's dead.

What's left of him.

What *is* left of him?

"What happened to him?" I ask, interrupting my dad.

"It's best you come here. We can talk in person."

"No, tell me now. I need to know."

"All that's left is his head. Whoever did this to him cut it off."

My blood runs cold, ice spiking through my body.

I can't hold the phone anymore and it slips from my hands, landing in the blankets. My father's voice sounds like it's coming from far away now.

"Neve? *Neve?* For fuck sakes. Be here at ten."

Silence.

He hung up.

I still can't move.

My hands are shaking so badly I clench them into tight fists, pushing my nails into the palm of my hands and trying to use the pain to pull myself back into my body.

I take in one sharp breath - and start crying.

Damion's dead.

I kept telling everyone that something bad had happened, but maybe I didn't believe that myself. Someone murdered him. It wasn't even an accident. People don't accidentally cut off other people's heads.

The nausea comes out of nowhere and I have to run for the bathroom.

Wave after wave I heave up every single thing left in my stomach. Bile burning my throat and the effort of puking causing my eyes to water.

At ten o'clock I march straight into my father's house, as numb as stone on the inside, I walk straight over to him and say, "It was Celso Vece." With all the force I can muster.

"Are you fucking crazy?" My father hisses, grabbing my arm, his fingers dig into my skin, and I think - later I'll be bruised.

I try to pull my arm away, but his grip is like steel as he pulls me into another room.

"There are fucking reporters everywhere. Why the fuck would you say something like that?" he whispers.

"Because Celso did something to Damion, dad. Believe me. He killed Damion. We can't let him get away with this. We have to go to the police."

Tears are flowing freely down my cheeks while I speak.

My father sets one sharp slap across my face, and it freezes all of my emotions in place.

I stare at him in disbelief.

He lifts his finger and points it right into my face.

"You don't dare breathe a word of this pathetic idea to anyone. Do you understand me? I don't want to hear a single fucking thing about this again." He's furious.

"Are we going to let him get away with murder?" I plead.

My father snarls.

"Dad, if you listen—" he slaps me again and I bite the inside of my lip, the sharp metallic taste of blood touches my tongue.

"Not - a - fucking - word - Neve." My father says, spelling each work out for me with the way he is enunciating them.

I stare at him.

"Do you understand?" he shakes me.

I nod.

"Get a hobby. Stop thinking stupid thoughts." He mutters, releasing me and walking away.

I stare after him with so much anger inside me I can't move.

Anger and confusion and grief.

Damion didn't deserve this.

Who would have done this to him?

I can't think of anyone but Celso.

For the longest time I just stand there, not knowing what to do because I can't talk to anyone about it, and I can't face any reporters that my father has lined up and I still can't move.

"Neve?" A soft voice draws my attention, and I look up to see one reporter. My heart sinks.

"Please, I don't want to answer questions." I stammer.

"I wanted to see if you were ok. I mean, it can't be easy." The girl walks into the room, standing close to me, tentatively she reaches out and wraps her arm around my shoulder.

"I—"

"It's ok, I can't imagine what you're going through." She says, and I lean my face against her shoulder, sobbing massive tears as I fall apart.

It took me about fifteen minutes to pull myself back together after I broke down.

My father came into the room, glared at me, and demanded that I attend the interview he'd set up. The reporter stepped away from me in a hurry and left the room and I was forced to pull myself together.

That was several hours ago.

Now I'm back home and watching myself on television. My eyes are red and swollen, and my face is blotchy on the screen.

I shrink down into my sofa, horrified about how bad I look, horrified that everyone is willing to brush this off and not discuss what is really going on and horrified that my father - knowing full well what the mafia is capable of - doesn't even want to consider that it might be true.

He's more worried about his campaign than Damion.

Damion is dead, my thoughts brutally remind me.

All that's left is his head.

Over the next three days I don't leave my apartment. I can't face the world outside.

On the news I watch the story unfold as they uncover bit by bit what happened to him.

A car is pulled out of a lake. The rest of his body is found in the car.

The medical guys speculate that his head was decapitated during an accident. I don't believe it for one second.

Cause of death is ruled accidental, and the world has a moment of mourning the story is over.

Just like that.

Everyone forgets Damion because it's no longer exciting anymore.

Another three days go past and I'm not sure what I'm supposed to do with myself. I'm falling apart. I'm lost. I'm worried.

And worse - *I'm still falling asleep thinking about Celso.*

What is wrong with me? I'm so attracted to the man I believe is a murderer?

CHAPTER TEN
Celso

The last time I saw Neve was when she told me that girls like her don't date guys like me. Now she's fallen off the map. The news has been going crazy after some local kids found her ex's head on the side of the road - and then the rest of his body.

Dalila has been complaining every time I've seen her at our family dinners - she keeps saying that Neve is hardly responding to her.

"Her fiancé died in an accident." Masaccio says, huffing slightly. "She needs time to process."

"An accident?" Dalila asks, knotting her brows.

"The news announced it last night. The coroner's report came back, and they said he was drunk and drove his car off the bridge into the river."

"And his head *fell off?*" Dalila asks in horror.

"Apparently he got half thrown from the car - his neck caught on the railing and his head went one way and his body fell back into the car." Tuomo shrugs, joining in the speculation.

"Oh, my word." Dalila huffs, looking like she wants to throw up.

"So, that's it. It was an accident." My father says, looking up from his newspaper.

"Sure. An accident." Mas mutters, glaring at me.

"Oh, fucking let it go, Masaccio." I hiss.

Technically everything should be over now.

The news will calm down, everyone will go back to their lives, and Neve and I can be together. Except she won't come out of her apartment. And she thinks I am a criminal with no future.

And that means that I have to put the rest of my plan into action. I have no choice. I have given her enough of a chance to come to me and she hasn't taken it.

So now it's time for me to give her no choice.

I always get what I want. She is going to find out soon.

A girl like her is about to find out she doesn't get to say no to a man like me.

When I get home, I head straight into the office across the hall from my bedroom.

Pulling my laptop open I type in an email address.

Attaching three videos and four very clear images I leave the subject line blank and hit send. The same email gets sent to two other addresses.

Now I have to sit back and wait.

My email is heavily encrypted.

They won't know who the source is - nor will they care. The photos are genuine, so is the video. I've been holding onto them for a long time waiting for a moment like this when they would come in useful.

Her father is going to be under a lot of pressure when the stories come out. Either tonight or tomorrow. I'm sure they will all scramble to be the first one to release the story - the truth is going to hit the media stands and his campaign will start to crumble.

Neve needs me more than she knows - but if I have to put some effort in to prove that to her - so be it.

The next morning the internet is absolute chaos. Every page of every social media site is plastered with images of her father. In some they have blurred his face out, but it's still so clearly him. The same videos play on repeat across the wild web.

Franco Greco with hookers, doing blow, partying up a storm. In one photo he's so fucking high I don't think he knows his own name. His eyes practically rolling into the back of his own skull while a hooker is between his legs.

I smirk at the mayhem I've created.

And over the next few days I watch his campaign numbers plummet.

It's interesting to hear how his die-hard supporters try to justify his disgrace. *He's only human. We all deserve to let loose sometimes* - blah blah blah.

Their arguments make no difference.

His campaign is fucked and the strained faces of his family members and campaign managers as they try to scrape whatever dignity the man still has off the floor - it's amusing. His son, the one who's still alive, is hustling to help his father - but it's too late.

His time is up.

I push away from my laptop where I've been catching up on the latest news and numbers. I should get ready. It's getting late and I don't want to miss anything.

Tonight, I have a family dinner at Dalila's house, and I hope to get some inside information on how Neve is handling all of this. I need to remain tactful in my questions because Dalila is already pissed off at me every time, I even mention her friend's name.

Apart from getting an update on Neve, I don't want to go to the dinner. I'm not in the mood to sit around talking about their lives and how great everyone is. It's boring.

Except, when I arrive at my sister's place and spot Neve standing outside on the patio holding a gin in her hand and talking to Masaccio - the entire night shift.

My eyes take in the sight of her, the long blue dress she's wearing, how it dips low over her back showing off the delicate curve of her spine. Her hair is pinned up in a messy bun with loose waves drifting around her face. The fabric of her dress and those strands of hair are dancing on a gentle breeze.

Now I want nothing more than to be here.

In fact - I wouldn't choose to be anywhere else on this entire fucking planet.

"Hi, Cels." Dalila says cheerfully when I walk past her in the living room.

"Hi." I mutter without looking at her, making a straight line towards Neve.

"Hey, that's rude." Dalila huffs. I catch myself quickly, realizing I need to be a lot more subtle when Dalila is around, I walk over to her and hug her tightly. "Sorry. My head is all fuzzy today. I've been working nonstop and I'm dying for a drink."

Dalila smirks. "Alright, fine, I'll forgive you this time." She hugs me back. "Can I make you a drink, I'm about to get one for Nevio."

"You're my favorite sister." I chuckle. "A whiskey - on the rocks." I say, following her to the outside bar on the patio. "I'm your only sister, smartass." She laughs.

My eyes are constantly tugging towards Neve. It's difficult not to stare at her the entire time.

"Here you go." She says, handing me a glass filled with golden liquid. Three enormous ice blocks clinking against the sides. "Single Malt - Thanks. How have you been? You look stressed."

"I've been good. Focused on trying to help Neve. You do not know how hard it was to convince her to come out tonight. She's been holed up in her apartment. I think she's overwhelmed by everything."

"With her father?" I ask, doing my best to sound casual.

"That - and it all happened right after the thing with Damion. She's so stressed out and I mean - who could blame her? "

"How is her dad doing?" I ask, pushing for more information.

"Horrible. She's pretty sure he's about to have a heart attack." Dalila sighs in frustration.

"He was an idiot for doing such stupid things." I shrug.

"I know - I know - but still - I feel bad about how it's affecting Neve. I wish I could help her. Her brother is trying to convince her father to step down so that he can take over the campaign. To save something of their family name. But her father is so freaking stubborn, and bull headed - and besides, with all the PR recovery I think they're running out of funds. I don't know what they're going to do."

"It's not a bad idea for her brother to take over, start fresh with the campaign." In fact, it was exactly what I was counting on. They are going to need help soon. And I will be there to clean up the mess her father left, financially they will need my support more now than ever.

"Well, you try telling that to her dad. He's more stubborn than our old man." She smirks, raising her brows, making me chuckle.

"Oh dammit, I forgot Nevio was waiting for his drink." Dalila giggles and hurries away, leaving me standing alone by the bar watching Neve.

Her conversation with Mas ends, and he excuses himself, walking towards his wife, Leora. But not before gently touching Neve's arm and squeezing softly. It makes me angry to see his hands on her. He has no right to touch her.

Before anyone else has a chance to move towards her, I make my way there.

As I come closer, I can smell that gorgeous scent of hers. Intoxicating as always.

"I'm sorry for what's happening with your father." I say, stepping close to her side.

"I'm sure you're devastated." She snaps back sarcastically.

"Why would you say it like that?" I ask, the corner of my mouth turning up ever so slightly.

"Was it you?" she asks, her eyes turns fiercely onto me. Her lashes lowered as she narrows her gaze at me.

"Was *what* me, my angel? You're going to have to be a lot more specific than that."

She pulls her mouth tight, biting her lower lip and huffing.

"Did you leak the photos? The videos?" She speaks clearly.

I knit my brows, looking hurt by her accusation.

"Neve, my family has supported your father's campaign for years. What benefit would I have in doing something like that?" She shakes her head, unable to answer.

Neve's eyes lower and she swirls her gin in its glass, shifting uncomfortably.

"Did you - kill Damion?" she asks, barely a whisper.

I reach out, letting my hand rest on her slender waist. The heat of her body searing through me. One simple touch and I could get lost in her.

"You've been through a lot lately. Your fiancé was in that horrible accident, and now your father's - *private activities* - have been made public. I want you to know that if you ever need to talk to someone - or for someone to be there for you - you can call me. Anytime of the day or night."

She glares at me but doesn't step away from my touch.

"I don't want your help, Celso. I want to know what is going on." She snaps.

"Neve, I've told you before, but perhaps you need to be reminded." I say, stepping a little closer to her and lowering my voice. Our bodies brush against each other even so, she doesn't step away from my touch.

Her bright blue eyes are wide as she stares up at me. Her lip's part and she takes in a sharp breath.

"What?" she whispers.

"I love you, and you belong to me. That means that you can ask me for anything, and I will be there for you."

Her cheeks flush rose pink.

She clears her throat and lets out a puff of air as though she's been holding her breath.

"I don't want your help." She stammers, stepping away from me. I drop my hand from her waist and notice her shudder.

Without looking at me she walks away.

I chuckle as she hurries towards the bar to refill her drink that isn't even half finished.

I've unsettled her.

I love that glint in her eyes. Confirmation that she feels it too. Confirmation that she loves my hand on her skin.

"Soon, my angel. Soon." I whisper a promise to her as I lift my whiskey to my lips.

CHAPTER ELEVEN
Neve

My father is pacing up and down his living room. My brother and him have been going at it, arguing about everything, for about an hour. I'm exhausted. I haven't said a word, and I don't think they even realize I'm still here.

"Franco, you need to think about the numbers. They are lower than they've ever been. Before it's too late, we need to do something drastic to recover them."

Luke always calls my father by his first name. The only time he calls him Dad is when he's doing some family interview and wants to appear sensitive.

"I said no." My father snaps angrily. "I can fix this."

"How?" Luke asks with desperation flooding from his lips.

If I was allowed to have any opinion in this matter, I would side with Luke. My father's campaign has tanked. It's below rock bottom and even if Luke takes over now, it might not be salvageable. Our family is out of money, the bank accounts are bled dry, most of the campaign members have walked out - things are bad. Like seriously bad.

I don't even read the news anymore because it's too embarrassing to know those things about my father and to hear other people share their very unwanted opinions on the matter.

"I've asked the campaign manager to mortgage the house." My father mutters, talking to himself, not us. "When that money comes through, we can restart the campaign - come in from a fresh angle—"

Luke bursts out laughing. "You've bonded the house? Is that a joke?" He snarls.

My father shoots him a glare filled with heated anger.

"Franco, there is no money in the house. You used it all up - probably not even on the campaign but on hookers and cocaine." He throws his hands in the air.

"Don't you dare talk to me like that, boy!" My father snarls and my brother takes a step back. He nods and sighs, pushing his hand through his slick black hair.

"Sorry." He mutters. "I'm stressed."

"We are all stressed."

If my father won't let Luke take over, I don't see a way out of this. Our family is - for lack of a better word - fucked. We will lose the house, the cars, the status we have in the community. I don't even know if I care about all of that anymore. What was the point of it? It got us to this point. A son who calls his father by his first name. A father who views his kids as media props - a little perfect family of cut out dolls to put on display as needed. We are hardly a family at all.

I miss my mother.

I miss her more than anything right now.

In fact, if I think back, my dad only became this way after the cancer stole her from us fifteen years ago. He was never this cold before that.

The thought breaks my heart. My dad became this way to numb himself. To distract himself from losing the woman he loved dearly.

I stand up and walk over to him.

"Dad?" I say gently.

He turns to look at me with surprise in his eyes. "Neve?" He replies,

"Dad, I think you need to take a few breaths and calm down for a while. The doctor already warned you that your blood pressure was through the roof. You need to sit - for a bit." I gently touch his arm and try to lure him towards the sofa. "I can make you some tea."

"I don't fucking want any tea, girl. I want to sort out this fucking mess."

I cringe away from him. My brother shakes his head.

"Neve's right. You're going to give yourself a stroke." He snaps at my father and storms from the room.

Knowing my father became this way after losing my mother doesn't make it any easier to deal with emotionally when he treats me like shit.

I am so desperate for a hug, an embrace, a kind word. Some kind of softness from him that lets me know the man who raised me is still in there somewhere and not only this hard-shelled political robot.

Everything is falling apart around me, my entire life crumbling, and I don't know how to fix it. I'm still grieving the murder of my fiancé - yes. Murder. I don't care what the news said. I think he was killed.

And I think Celso had something to do with those photos of my father being leaked.

And no one will listen to me about it.

But what good would it do, anyway?

It wouldn't bring Damion back.

It wouldn't undo the leaked images.

Things would still be a total shit show.

Maybe everything should fall apart. Maybe we need to lose everything.

Along with the house and the constant media attention - I would also lose the overbearing rules that have been drowning me for the last fifteen years. I could live my life instead of living my father's life. His version of who I should be and what I should do.

I can't sit here anymore. I'm driving myself crazy and there is no point in all of us going crazy.

"I need air." I mutter, walking out of the living room.

As though she reads my mind - Dalila phones.

"Hi." I say tightly.

"Oh wow, is it that bad?" She asks.

"It's worse. I don't know how to handle this, and he won't listen to anyone he's so freaking stubborn."

"I know all about stubborn. Meet me at DaVinci."

"Now?" I look around myself as though I have to ask for permission from someone.

"Yip. Fifteen minutes."

"I'll be there." The best thing for me to do right now is to get out of here and clear my head. I can't help with any of this because they won't let me, and it's driving me insane.

I don't bother telling anyone - I head out to my car and start making my way into town. If they need me, they can call me - but I know they won't.

DaVinci is a quaint restaurant near the docks. It overlooks the water and serves the most amazing pasta dishes. The real deal. And the best, rich strong coffee. They roast their own beans and the moment I walk through the doors into the restaurant that is what I can smell.

Fresh coffee.

I arrive before Dalila and find a seat near the windows.

Opening my phone, I flick through social media for a second, regretting it because everything is horrible, and set my phone face down on the table.

I think better of it, and I put my phone in my bag. I don't even want to look at it. It's a portal to mayhem and chaos.

Dalila slides into the seat opposite mine and grins at me.

"You look terrible." She smirks.

"Well - gee - thanks." I shake my head, but the moment she arrives I'm smiling. She has that way about her. Some friends are like medicine, you can spend five minutes with them, and you feel better - Dalila is that friend.

A server comes over and stares down at us with an expectant smile.

I pick up the menu. "Ah—" I stammer, not in the mood to make choices.

Dalila eyes me, raises one brow and looks at the server.

"We'll have a bottle of the house white, semi-sweet. One mushroom risotto and one tagliatelle butternut and pistachios."

"Would you like a cream sauce on the side?"

"Yes. Thanks. And please hurry with the wine. You can even put a second bottle on ice for us."

The server nods and takes our menus from us.

"Thank goodness for you. It would have taken me an hour to figure out what I wanted to eat."

"I know, I can see that look in your eye."

"What look?" I laugh.

"The one that says - *if someone makes me think my head might explode.*"

I sigh and press my fingers into my temple. "My head might explode."

She reaches across the table and takes my hand. "Hey, it's going to be ok. No matter what happens - it'll be ok in the end. Your father's actions are his own, Neve."

"He's such a difficult man, but he's still my father."

"Don't worry - I know exactly how that is." She smirks, rolling her eyes.

The wine arrives and after the server has poured us each a glass Dalila lifts hers and touches it against the edge of mine.

"To the best friend in the world."

I nod. "To you." I smile.

"How lucky am I?" A smooth, rich voice brushes over my skin and runs down my spine like a heat wave. Turning I find Celso standing next to our table looking as divine as ever.

He pulls the chair out and sits himself down.

Dalila rolls her eyes. "I didn't invite you to sit. What are you doing here anyway - you hate this place? You said it wasn't Italian enough." She snickers.

Celso ignores his sister's taunts and reaches out to gently tuck a loose strand of hair behind my ear. "You look as beautiful as ever."

My cheeks flush bright pink and I turn my face away from him, knowing I can't hide it, but trying to. I lift my wine glass and sip it because I desperately need something to do.

My heart is racing at his touch, my eyes wanting to roam over his shapely lips and stare into those perfect blue eyes.

"What the hell?" Dalila mutters, her brows knotted.

Celso sits back, his legs spread wide as he relaxes in the chair. "What did you guys' order? The Risotto is the best thing on the menu."

"You're not invited Celso."

"Don't be mean, Dalila." He chuckles.

"But seriously, what are you doing here?" she demands.

I stare at him, watching the dimples form on his cheeks when he smiles, and the sculpted shape of his jaw. He looks calm and confident as he rolls the sleeves of his shirt up over his taunt, muscular forearms. My eyes trace across his broad shoulders and now all I'm thinking about is that kiss -

"Neve?" Dalila says in frustration. "Are you on planet earth?"

"Sorry, I'm exhausted - I spaced out for a second."

"Yeah, you were staring at my brother like he was a chunk of birthday cake." She huffs.

I chuckle. I could eat him up.

What the hell, Neve. He's a dangerous, possibly murderous arrogant asshole. No one is eating anyone up. Get a grip.

"I was telling my brother that it's a *girl's* lunch."

I bite my lip. I want him to stay - but that is the exact reason he needs to leave.

"Yip, sorry, no boys allowed." I say, sassy and full of attitude. Someone needs to bring him down a notch or two, anyway.

Celso chuckles. But I can see the rejection in his face. It bothers me I made him feel that way - which is crazy - but he stands up and nods towards the food the server is busy setting down in front of us.

"I'm sure you ladies will enjoy it."

He leans over and kisses Dalila on the cheek and she pulls a face.

He leans over and kisses me on the cheek, and I freeze, my face flushing red again as the dark delicious scent of his cologne washes over me. "Neve," he whispers.

Then he leaves and Dalila is staring at me like I have a lobster on my head.

"What the hell was that?" She snaps.

"What?" I mutter.

"Is there something going on between you and my brother?" she demands.

"No. Ewe. Celso is too - creepy." I say, trying to sound like I mean it. "I know the rules, Dalila. I wouldn't do that to you. I wouldn't risk our friendship like that."

She nods, satisfied with my answer.

I wouldn't do it. I tell myself.

CHAPTER TWELVE
Celso

"It should have been *you* he killed instead of your mother. It's the only reason he favors you so much - because he regrets what he did to her." Masaccio spits.

"Masaccio! *What the fuck?*" Tuomo hisses.

"We've all thought it at one point." Mas snaps.

"My *mother*?" I ask, barely a whisper. "He killed her?"

"No man, it's a stupid rumor." Tuomo glares at Masaccio with an intensity I don't understand.

"Did our father *kill* my mother?" I ask darkly.

Masaccio runs his hands through his hair and squeezes his eyes shut for a second.

"No. Sorry. Uh. I was trying to piss you off." Masaccio is backing off, clenching his jaw as he turns his back on me.

We are all in my father's living room even though he is away on business. Tuomo stands up, walking over to me. "Mas is confused why dad is sending you to talk to Franco Greco instead of him, as the oldest in the family and the next in line to take over - it just - it didn't make sense."

"Greco is a key part of how we run this city. If you fuck up this meeting, you fuck up a lot of other things for the family." Mas growls. "And it's already all a fuck up - did you leak those photos?" He stares at me accusingly.

"Oh, fuck off." I snarl.

Masaccio doesn't know that I pleaded with my father to let me represent him at this meeting with Greco while he's out of town - because I have something else, I want to present to the man.

But what Mas said is all I can think about.

Did my father kill my mother?

A crime of passion?

A crime of hate?

They are so closely interlinked it could be either or both.

I shake the thought from my head. It can't be. My father loves me because he loved my mother. He always regretted it when she left. I think if he could have, he would have chosen her over his wife.

But maybe that's why he had to kill Amelia.

His wife, Francesca, his family, the kids - in Cosa Nostra you don't abandon your family for your mistress. And maybe her death was the only thing that could seal his choice not to be with her?

My heart churns. I might understand that - if that happened.

He killed her because he couldn't have her and the thought of her still being out there - with someone else - he couldn't live with it.

But - did my father take my mother from me? All these years - did he do that?

"Celso." Mas snaps. "I *said* this is *important*."

"Yeah, for fuck sakes. I heard you. I know what to say. I know how to fucking handle my business, Masaccio." I snarl, turning my back on him. He's an arrogant fuck. Right now, I can't even look at him. "I'm leaving." I snap, heading for the door.

Before I close it behind me, I hear Tuomo. "What the actual fuck, Masaccio?"

Driving towards Franco Greco's place I'm thinking about Neve.

She was still off with me when I bumped into her at DaVinci yesterday. Obviously, I knew they were because I followed her there.

She's still fighting me though. Not giving in to what is going on between us.

That's fine.

I'm done playing nice and giving her the choice. At this point it's time for the men to negotiate and she will have to fall in line and do as she's told.

One of Greco's campaign guys is waiting for me when I climb out of my car.

"Mr. Vece, Mr. Greco is ready for you in the sunroom. If you will follow me." He gestures with his hand towards the high arched entrance of Greco's over the top mansion. The man likes luxury, that's clear. I'm hoping that pushes him to say yes to my proposal. He wouldn't want to lose all of this - and all of his other little luxuries.

"Thank you." I nod towards the guy and follow him through the house, up the stairs and into the sunroom where Greco is standing by the window, his hands clasped behind his back.

He doesn't turn to look at me when I walk in. Luke, his son, is sitting by the sofas. He nods at me politely.

"Mr. Vece, sir." The guy announces my arrival.

"Vincent - I can't thank you enough for—" Franco turns and his face falls.

"My father is away on business, so I am here to represent the family and our business relationship with you." I say, taking a seat, folding one leg across the other and sitting with my arms draped on each armrest.

I stare at Franco with a smirk.

"I'd rather deal directly with your father." He says, looking nervous and angry.

"Well, you have me. If that's not good enough for you perhaps you would like to find another mafia familia to fund your bad habits?"

Greco's mouth pulls tight as he walks towards me and sits down in the chair opposite.

"Can I get you a drink?" he asks, tense and polite.

"No, thank you. I'd like to get straight to business."

"Good. Yes."

Franco Greco is a wreck. His eyes are sunken beneath dark circles. He looks exhausted and he won't stop fidgeting. He keeps clenching his jaw and biting at the inside of his cheek. His eyes are darting left and right, unable to focus on anything.

"Franco, we can help you solve this mess. We can put enough money towards your campaign to recover your standing with the public. We have the access to the best PR team, and you won't have to worry about a thing. Just show up when they tell you and do what they ask."

Franco's eyes dart onto me, glimmering with hope. "You can do that?" he stammers.

"We can do that." I nod, reassuringly. "But you have to do something for me in return. For my family."

"What?" he says, tensing again. Whenever it comes time to return the favors, these types of men suddenly clench up. They are all the same. Happy to take, take and take - and they act shocked when you ask them for something in return.

Luke shifts in his seat but hasn't said a word - as though his father forbade him from doing anything but being present.

"What is it we can help you with?" Franco asks tightly.

"Your daughter, Neve, will marry me." I say - as clear as day. Leaving no room for misunderstanding.

"What the fuck?" Franco leaps from his chair and glares at me in anger. "Are you fucking insane? Neve isn't going to marry into the mafia - then - are you?" He clasps his hand over his chest and starts to breathe heavily. "My - daughter - will never - marry - I'll never - allow it."

Luke stands up, unsure what to do.

He rushes to his father's side.

I stand up as well. Angered by his reaction. His disgust. His distaste. His disrespect.

"I'll give you some time to think about it. But unless you agree to that we will not be helping you with your campaign again." I say stiffly, with one last look at Franco as he gasps and clutches his chest, fighting for air - I leave. Luke's eyes are on me when I leave, I can feel them, heated against my back.

I chuckle as I walk out of Franco's house, savoring his shock, enjoying his torment. He knows he has no other options. Either his campaign tanks or his daughter marries me. But his reaction tells me he might choose the wrong option. He might let his campaign die in order to not give away his daughter.

I sneer, angry again, as I climb into my car.

He looked terrible and I've obviously added stress to an already stressful situation. All I can do now is wait. Wait - and hope that the universe proves to me that Neve and I are together by making it possible.

My phone buzzes as messages come through from my father.

> Vincent: How did the meeting go?
>
> Me: He's considering our offer and will get back to me by tomorrow afternoon.

Of course, my father knows nothing about what I have set as a requirement in the offer.

This morning I might have felt guilty over this, keeping things from my father when it comes to business - but ever since Masaccio slipped up and told me that small, *insignificant* truth - the truth about what he did to my mother. Well, let's say I don't give a shit about what he wants anymore.

> Vincent: They like to pretend they have a choice and that they are in charge of the situation. Let him take his time, but he always chooses the same thing. He'll take the money. He knows we own him.

Except this time, I don't think he's going to. The way he responded was a lot more intense than I expected it to be. He was adamant that he would not agree to his daughter marrying me. Well, if that is the case he will lose everything.

The guy practically had a panic attack though.

"Fuck." I shout, slamming my hands against the steering wheel.

If this plan doesn't work, I might kidnap her. Fuck it. It's not ideal - but what choice do I have? She is *mine. She belongs to me, and she should be with me.*

I take a few deep, slow breaths, forcing myself to calm down.

I can't act rashly now. Not after I've been so patient for so long.

The universe wants us to be together.

It will make it happen.

And that evening - my theory is proven.

The universe does want us to be together.

I pick up the remote control and turn the volume on the TV up.

"Mr. Franco Greco, the man who was head of the polls for the last three years running, has passed away of an apparent heart attack this afternoon. We are just hearing that his son, Luke, was by his side at the time of his death. Luke has a few words to say to our viewers."

The screen switches to an image of Luke, Neve standing by his side outside their father's home. "My sister and I are devastated by this loss. We ask you all to respect our privacy and grief during this time, but I also want you to know that I will be taking over his campaign and working very hard to recover our family name. What my father did, his choices and his actions, are not a reflection of our family. He acted alone and we hope that all the people who supported his campaign understand I still believe in everything it stood for. I want to make our people proud...."

I flick the mute button and while Luke's mouth continues to move, no sound comes out.

"Greco - you were too weak." I chuckle, sitting down on the sofa and still watching Luke silently make his plea to his kingdom to allow him to run for office.

Politics.

I sit back, spreading my legs out and draping my arms over the back of the sofa. So, Luke Greco is the new man of the house. He is the one who will make the choices now.

And he is the man who I am going to be negotiating with.

I wonder what he thinks of my idea.

CHAPTER THIRTEEN
Neve

I pull the curtain closed angrily.

"They are still out there." I say. frustrated at their heartlessness.

"The reporters will always chase the story, Neve." Luke says, not sounding bothered in the least. "Besides, our family needs sympathy now. If the media can give us that my campaign might take off again." He huffs.

"Are you fucking kidding me?" I shout. "That's all you care about. The media, the campaign, what people think - you sound like dad and look where that got him." Tears well up in the back of my eyes and then flood down my cheeks. I can't believe Luke is talking about this when our father only died two days ago - and since then the media has *not* been sympathetic.

I pick up yesterday's newspaper and slam it down on the table in front of Luke.

"Hey, I'm trying to work here." He snaps.

"Does that look like sympathy to you?" I growl, pointing at the front-page article about my father and the massive amounts of debt he was actually in - showing how deep his bad habits went. We had no idea. We didn't know he was into hookers, drugs, or gambling. But his bank accounts and the trust accounts and - well - our entire lives - are now fucked.

He took everything from us and died, leaving us with less than nothing.

"We are going to be homeless in less than a month if I don't pull something together for this campaign." Luke shouts angrily. "Can't you see that. We don't have any other options, Neve. This is it. This is our way out."

"Bullshit. Politics destroyed this family. I say we sell everything - clear the debt - take whatever little we have left over and start again. We don't have to have this big, crazy life, stalked by cameras every time we blink - we can be normal."

Luke laughs.

"We will never be normal, Neve. Do you really want that, anyway? A boring life. A quiet life?"

I sigh, brushing away my tears with the palm of my hand. "I want - I don't want *this.*" I gesture towards the window, the closed curtains hiding fifty reporters camped outside the house.

"Well, you have this, and you have to learn to deal with it." Luke snaps.

I shake my head. He's exactly like my father. Identical. Cold. Using the campaign to numb any emotions he might dare to feel.

I walk over to my brother and place my hand on his shoulder.

"Don't do what dad did, ok." I sigh, squeezing his shoulder.

"What do you mean?" he asks, abrupt and annoyed.

"Don't forget that you have people who love you.

Don't get so lost in the campaign that it's the only thing you care about."

He brushes my hand off his shoulder. "Grow up, Neve. Look around. It's too late for that. We are about to lose *everything*." He shouts.

"Not everything. We still have each other."

He huffs, an indignant snort. "What good is that if we are living on the streets?"

"Luke—"

"Leave me alone. I need to work. You aren't helping anything."

"If there was something I could do you know I would do it." I say tightly.

"Is that so?" he asks. His brows raise.

"I've always wanted to help with the campaigns. Dad never let me."

"Well, I might take you up on that offer." Luke says. his eyes turned down towards his laptop. The way he says it makes my skin crawl.

I'm losing my brother.

Sighing I shake my head. I lost my brother years ago when my father started grooming him to be who he is right now. Ruthlessly committed to the campaign.

"I'm going out." I mutter, grabbing my handbag from the edge of the table where he's sitting. He doesn't reply. He doesn't look at me. I am invisible to him. Like I don't matter at all.

I wish someone would see me. For me. Not for what role I can play in the media to make our family look better. Just for *me*. *A living breathing person with dreams and ideas and* - a heart.

A heart that wants nothing more than to be loved.

As I walk back towards my car, ignoring the reporters' screaming questions from outside the security gates, I think about Damion. Our marriage would not have lasted long. He is another cog in the political wheel. There was no love there. I tried to pretend. I tried to convince myself because I so desperately wanted my life to experience some joy. Something that was only for me. *A man who adored me.* But I knew he was not that man and somewhere inside me I also accepted that the marriage would be a nightmare. A clinical, strategic nightmare of a life. The perfect wife. The perfect marriage. But on the inside, it would be cold and heartless.

I tug my door open and climb into the car.

I want passion. I want to feel something. I want someone who would fight for me, who would do crazy things to win me over and to keep me and to make me smile.

I want - *Celso*.

I shake my head, sighing as I start the engine.

I'm losing my mind.

I've lost my father. I've lost my brother. I'm so utterly alone.

I slam my hand against the hooter and rev the car, letting it jerk forward when the reporters won't get out of the way so I can leave.

They are pressed up against my windows like savages. Cameras and microphones pointed at me. I rev again and think 'fuck this' as I slam the car into gear and drive.

Someone screams and people jump out of the way. I laugh as I escape their lockdown of bodies.

Glancing in the rearview mirror I can see everyone is fine, flustered and taken by surprise. Good. They are vultures. Nothing more.

I drive, not having any idea where I'm going - I want to get away from here. Somewhere far. Somewhere where no one knows me.

Of course, that's impossible. People know my face several states over. I could drive for three days straight and not be anonymous.

My phone beeps and I glance at the screen.

A message from an anonymous number. Someone not in my phone book.

> Unknown: I miss you. Are you doing, ok? I'm sorry about what happened to your father.

I grab the phone and type a quick response, knowing that driving and texting is a terrible idea.

> Me: Who is this?

> Unknown: The man who you belong to. The only man in the world who can make you happy.

I shake my head, but I'm grinning. The audacity of this man is astounding. He is relentless. It's like he refuses to give up no matter what is happening around him.

Pulling over to the side of the road because now I'm way too distracted to drive, I type my reply.

> Me: Celso, how did you even get this number?

> Celso: Anything is easy to find when you want it badly enough.

> Me: You can't always get what you want. That's not how the world works.

Why am I smiling so much?

> Celso: Watch me, angel. I always get what I want. And what I want is you.

I toss my phone onto the passenger seat, forcing myself to end this conversation. I can't play games like this. I can't flirt with him. He's not good for me.

But my heart is beating too fast and I'm smiling so much my cheeks are hurting.

My phone chimes again and I can't resist. I pick it up to read his message.

> Celso: Meet me somewhere. We can go for coffee. We can just talk. I promise I will behave.

I bite down hard on my lip. Don't do it, Neve. Don't do it -

But it's too late. I've already hit send.

> Me: Pier seven. The one near the big red lighthouse.

> Celso: I'm on my way, angel.

Fuck. What am I doing? Oh, my fuck this is so bad.

I push the car into gear and head towards pier seven. My heart is fluttering with a thousand butterflies, my stomach is a tight knot of excitement. I haven't felt this way since my first crush in junior high. Tingling and happy. He makes me feel so wanted. So desired.

He makes me feel like he would do anything to win me over.

And right now - even if it's for today - one stupid choice - I need it. I need it more than anything.

Keeping an eye on my rearview mirror to make sure no one is following me, I don't need some asshole reporter grabbing photos of me secretly meeting Celso, I take the long way to pier seven.

By the time I arrive Celso is already there, leaning against his car, casual and cool, looking as sexy as ever in a pair of jeans and a tight black t-shirt that hugs his body and shows off how sculpted he actually is.

I park and he opens my door for me.

"Hi gorgeous." He says seductively, holding his hand out for me to take.

I let him help me out of the car, but he doesn't let go of my hand - instead, he tugs me right up against his chest. He slips his arm around my waist and grabs the back of my head - and he kisses me. My brain is screaming at me not to do this, but my body is melting against his. I've been going through so much. I've been drawing in stress and worry and media and tension - and suddenly all I feel is calm.

His kiss is like a blanket of silence and safety that gets wrapped around me. His arm is like a weighted security locked around my body. His touch is a warmth I am so desperate to have.

His lips move against mine and I forget everything else.

It's only this.

Only now.

Celso breaks off the kiss and leans back to stare into my soul with those gorgeous blue eyes.

"You promised you would behave." I whisper.

He chuckles, stepping away from me completely. My body feels cold where he is no longer pressed against it. "I did. I promised that didn't I. Sorry." He grins.

I want to reach out and pull him back towards me, but I don't. I'm already playing with fire. I can't be throwing gasoline around.

"There's a little taco stand around the corner from here. Walk with me." He says, holding his hand out. I hesitate for a moment before I place my hand in his. *Just for today, Neve. Because you need this. You are allowed to feel this, only for today.*

I've never spent proper time with Celso before. Not alone, not one on one. I've never really taken the time to get to know him - for obvious reasons. Firstly, he is my best friend's brother. Secondly, he is a murderous, dangerous criminal from the underworld.

But this afternoon I have to admit that I'm surprised.

Maybe it's because I'm so desperate for attention - but he is warm, caring and genuine. He makes me laugh and to my utter shock, he seems sensitive and giving.

I don't know if he's fantastic at faking things to get what he wants - or if I'm seeing a side of him, I never knew existed. Either way, I go with the flow and let myself be lured by him.

Only for today.

CHAPTER FOURTEEN
Celso

I never intended for her father to die.

But it turns out it is exactly what needed to happen for things to start falling into place for us.

Yesterday Neve and I spent the day together and I have never felt so intensely and beautifully connected to another person in my entire life.

She is even more perfect than I could ever have imagined.

It was the perfect day with the perfect girl. The girl who already belongs to me. The one I will marry.

Unfortunately, after I said goodbye and arrived back home - I messaged her - and she seemed cold and distant again. It's frustrating how I'm getting closer to my goals, but then they drift a little further away again. One step forward, two steps back.

My phone rings and I rush to answer it, hoping it's her.

"Hello?" I say, not seeing her number.

"This is Luke Greco, I was hoping we could meet at some point today to discuss the campaign." He is sharp, polite, and tense.

My heart flips and a nervous current of energy bolts through me like sharp knives.

"Luke, good to hear from you. I am free this afternoon. I can come over in the next hour."

He swallows. "Good." He says. "I'll see you later. Thank you."

"Thank *you*." I smile, and hang up.

Well, would you look at that? Perhaps things aren't two steps back after all. Perhaps her father's death happened for more than one reason. Luke knows what I demanded of Franco in order to fund the campaign. Surely, he would not be calling a meeting with me if it wasn't to accept that deal?

I can barely contain myself. I can't think straight I'm so flooded with excitement. Is it happening? Pacing up and down my penthouse I try to calm myself down but it's not working. I'm so happy that I'm agitated. My skin is crawling, burning - I'm uncomfortable in my body.

I have to move.

Grabbing my keys, I know if I leave now, I'll get there too early. But I can take the long way around the city. A drive will be good for me. I want to arrive in control of myself, not like this.

Outside there is a light drizzle falling from the pale grey sky. It's still warm, and the rain makes the air smell fresh, washed clean of the past. It's a new beginning.

I climb into the car and start the engine, wondering what our wedding will be like, quickly stopping those thoughts because I have to stay neutral until I find out what he really wants. For all I know he might be trying another bargain. Another option. He does not know how much is at stake for me here - how badly I want his sister and how absolutely no other thing he might offer me will be considered.

I drive like a grandma crawling along to kill time, making my way through busy streets as people run around beneath black umbrellas with long coats covering their bodies. I'm smiling the entire way.

My fingers drumming in time to the music, beating out the tunes onto my steering wheel.

The wipers move in slow motion over the windshield, and I take a deep breath now and then to maintain the calm demeanor I've found.

Patience always pays off, Celso. And you always get what you want.

It's an hour after our phone call when I park outside his father's house. His house.

Luke, unlike his father, comes downstairs to greet me himself. Perhaps he didn't have a choice. Perhaps his campaign team has abandoned him, and he doesn't have any little minions running around taking care of his needs.

"Luke." I greet him, shaking his hand with a tight grip.

"Celso." He replies stiff and tense.

He gestures for me to follow him into the living room. We sit. He pours me whiskey from the bottle on the coffee table.

"I wanted to discuss the campaign with you - and uh - how we might get the funding going again. I plan to run it differently from how my father did, but the same principles will apply."

I take the whiskey and sip it, savoring the flavor and leaning back in the sofa.

Eyeing Luke I stare right at him, letting him feel the intensity of my eyes on him. "You know my terms, Luke. They haven't changed."

He sighs, his elbows resting on his knees as he swirls the whiskey in the glass. It's not the first drink he's had today. His eyes are rimmed with a red tint and the lids are drooping.

"I was hoping there was something else you might be interested in. You know, we've gotten rid of the reporters that have been parked outside the house for days at a time. We don't want more media coverage with another wedding. There has to be something else—"

"There isn't." I say, making my point more than clear.

He nods.

"So, this is the price of your support. There is no other way around it?"

I stand up, getting ready to leave.

"Luke, I didn't drive out here for you to waste my time. I made myself clear when I met with your father, and I've made myself clear again. I am not interested in any other deals, there is nothing else I want from you at this point in time. I've stated my terms. Take them or leave them."

He stares at the ground, his fingers tight around the glass in his hands.

I shake my head. He's fucking with me. "Thank you for the drink. I'll show myself out." I snarl, disappointed and angry.

"I'll do it." He mutters.

I pause, standing frozen in place.

"Excuse me?"

"I'll agree to your terms. I'll do it. But you have to sit down and tell me exactly what you are going to be providing for the campaign. I want a guarantee that this will work - whatever your PR team has planned or whatever—" he stammers, looking up at me with heavy regret painted across his face.

"Alright." I say, sitting down again. "I can't tell you how the PR team will recover your campaign - that will be up to them. But what I can tell you is that we have used them in the past when we had media issues, and they proved to be beyond capable of solving even the most complicated situations.

He clenches his jaw. "What if it doesn't work?"

"It will work. But apart from that - it's your risk to take. Now do we have a deal or not?" I am tired of sitting here treating him like a child, pandering to his worries, reassuring him - I want an answer, and I want it now.

"We have a deal." He nods. "You can marry my sister in exchange for your help in recovering my campaign and getting me back in the running."

"Excellent." I say, grinning from ear to ear, not even trying to hide how fucking happy I am right now. I am going to marry Neve. I am getting the exact and *only* thing that I want in this world. Her.

"Excuse me *what*?" She shouts from the doorway. "What the fuck did you say?"

She's looking at her brother, ignoring me.

"Neve calm down." He sighs.

"I will not fucking calm down did you sell me to the fucking mafia for money?" she screams.

"Neve!" he shouts, standing up and glaring at her with his fists clenched. I don't like how he's talking to her. No one talks to my future wife like that.

"Sit down, Luke." I growl.

He glances at me and his body shifts from anger to nervousness. "Yeah. Uh. We need to talk calmly, Neve." He mutters, sitting down again.

I turn towards Neve. "This is the best way to help your family."

"Shut up." She snaps. "I'm not speaking to you - I'm speaking to my brother."

She marches straight towards him and stands glaring down at him. His weakness becomes apparent at this moment, the way he moves inward, away from her anger.

"Did you *sell me to the mafia for money?*" She asks, tears springing to her eyes. I can't see her face, but I can hear them in her voice. Her throat is tight, and her words are coming out jagged and distorted.

"Neve, it's the only way we can get out of this mess. If we don't do this, we lose everything. Literally everything. We will be living on the streets in a month. You've already lost your apartment and had to move back in here - how do you think this is going to get any better? You said you wanted to help. You said you would do whatever you could to help—"

I would never have let that happen. Perhaps her brother would have been living on the streets - but not her. She would have been living with me. I didn't know the situation was that bad though. It seems I was going to win either way.

"This isn't what I *meant*, Luke. Not *this*. I didn't want — she can't speak anymore. She turns and flops down onto the sofa next to her brother and puts her hands over her face, hiding the heavy flow of tears streaming down her cheeks.

"Neve, I assure you that you will be happy." I say.

"I will be happy?" she laughs. "Happy?" She shakes her head in disbelief. "You don't even know what makes me happy. You don't have a clue what I want for my life. What I dream of and what I hope for. You don't know anything about me." She shouts.

I stand up and walk over to her, crouching in front of her, I place my hand beneath her chin. "I know a lot more about you than you think. And what I don't know I will learn."

I stand up again.

It's best that I give her space to process this now. She can come to terms with it in her own time, but the wedding is happening. It's agreed. Nothing is going to stop it now.

Turning towards Luke I say, "I'll cover everything for the wedding as well. You won't need to do a thing. Just make sure your sister shows up. As soon as the wedding is over, I will ensure you have everything you need."

"Well, best we get things moving quickly then." He says, standing up to see me out.

"Don't get up. I'll see myself out."

He nods, unsure what to do with himself. I think he is scared to be alone with his sister after betraying her so deeply. She might be furious now, but this is the best thing that could happen. Soon she will see how incredible we are together. That we were always meant to be.

"I'll see you soon." I say to Neve, smiling, my eyes tracing over my future wife. She stares at me in bitter silence. Salty tears staining her skin.

Tilting my head to say goodbye, I turn to leave them in their shock and anger.

I have things to do. Things to arrange. I have a wedding to plan.

The lights on my car flash as I unlock it. I don't think I've ever been this happy in my life. Everything I have ever wanted - and it's about to come true.

Neve will have the most beautiful wedding in the world. I will make sure of it. It will be perfect.

CHAPTER FIFTEEN
Neve

I watch Celso walk out of the living room and head towards the front door.

My heart is beating so loudly it sounds like a thousand wild horses, their hooves hammering against the dirt in a thunderous roar.

My brother sold me.

He sold my life as though I was something to use, a tool to trade with. As though I was nothing.

He gave me away and didn't even care to ask me.

My heart is shattering. Splintering and breaking apart. The pain is too much to bear.

"Neve." Luke says, quiet and timid.

"Shut up." I blurt out, my voice still tight from crying. "I don't want to hear it. I hate you. I hate you for what you've done."

"But - you'll go through with it right? You'll marry him to save our family?"

It's still all he's focused on. He doesn't care if I'm ok. He doesn't care about me at all.

"I'll do it. But right now - you need to stay far away from me Luke." I warned him, standing up and glaring at him with eyes that might set fire to his skin. I want him to feel the pain I'm in. To know what it's like to have your own brother betray you like this.

But he looks away, not even man enough to hold my gaze.

I spin away from him and march out of the living room.

I march out of the entire house, out into the front yard.

"Hey." I shout at Celso.

He stops, turning, that divine smile across his lips.

"My angel." He says, making my heart flutter.

"What the fuck game do you think you are playing?" I demand angrily. "Who the hell do you think you are? You can't buy me? I'm not a car. I'm not somet*hing* you get to throw money at and own."

"Angel, that's not how I see it at all. You aren't a thing. You aren't a toy. You are the most precious and rare and beautiful creature on this planet, and I want to marry you. I want to make you my wife so that I can spend the rest of my life with you at my side."

I stammer, tripping over everything I had planned to say to him. I came out here to shout at him, to make sure he knows how angry I am. But his words have thrown me off. His tenderness is clouding my ability to think.

Celso steps close to me, the heat of his body brushing against mine and now I can't breathe. "I —" I stammer. "I'm not just—" But I can't remember what I wanted to say.

"You're everything, my angel." He whispers against my lips. His long fingers wrap around my jaw as he tilts my face upward. "Do you understand me?" he demands.

I nod, blindly.

His mouth locks over mine, his lips move against me. I gasp, a wild heat running through my entire body as I lean towards him. He pulls me closer with his hand against my lower back. He moves, spinning me and pressing my back against the side of the car. He kisses me harder, pressing his lips against mine with more urgency. His cock is like a chiseled stone against my stomach.

I want him. I want him to take me, right here, against the car. Fuck the world and what they think of me. Fuck the campaigns and the reporters.

Celso chuckles, a delicious smooth sound that runs over me like caramel.

"You have to wait, angel. Our wedding night is coming soon." He says, stepping back. My eyes drop to his cock and widen at the sheer size of it. I felt it, but seeing the outline pressed against his pants, running down his left thigh, I swallow hard. He laughs again.

"I'll see you soon." He says, spinning me away from the car and climbing inside. I can't move or speak or do freaking anything.

I'm furious and turned on - and more confused that I have ever been in my life.

What the fuck is going on right now?

Celso opens his window and reaches out to touch me, sparks shoot between us. "Go inside, beautiful girl." He says and I nod. "Ok." I mutter. Then, obediently I turn back towards the house and walk inside - wondering how he has the power to command me like that. The heat between my legs suggests he has a lot of power over me. A desire so intense I never dreamed it was possible to experience something like this.

I walk upstairs to my old bedroom and sit down on the edge of the bed, blinking at the wall, trying to come to terms with everything going on.

Am I going to marry Celso Vece?

And through my overwhelming anger - is that excitement pulsing beneath the surface? How ridiculous is this? It's too crazy.

I can't - I won't - I don't understand.

In the back of my mind a thought is teasing at me. It'll be a wild adventure. And I've been longing for freedom and something exciting. I've been longing to feel alive, to be loved and desired.

But this is too much.

I stand up, huffing and throwing my hands in the air. "I've lost my fucking mind." I say to no one.

"Neve?" Luke says, standing in the doorway. "Can we talk?"

I walk over to him, shooting knives from my eyes as I glare at him - and slam my bedroom door in his face.

No.

We can't talk.

I'm angry with him, but I'm even more angry with myself. Why did I let Celso get to me like that? I have to stay in control of myself if I'm going to find a way out of this. I don't want to be married. I want to be free. I want to live my life. After the whole thing with Damion happened, that was the main, glaring truth that I came to learn. I don't want to be tied into some contractual obligation.

And I really don't want to be attracted to Celso.

I flop down onto my bed, face-first, with my head buried in my pillows.

"What is going on?" I groan, rolling onto my back.

Later the same night, lying on my bed again and scrolling through my phone, I am horrified to find an article about my apparent engagement online. It's suggestive and alluring and hints at some mysterious love that has been growing amongst the chaos of everything else. It doesn't flat out announce our engagement - but it's a very suggestive article. A teaser - basically. There are two separate images. One of me and one of Celso. Ugh. So prim and proper. It's a photo of me from one of my father's campaign events. I hate it. It's not who I am.

It's clear from this that Celso is building up to the big reveal. From the looks of things, he's loving this. And dammit he looks so freaking good in that photo.

Not a moment after I finish reading the article, rolling my eyes every five minutes, my phone rings.

"Dalila." I say nervously.

"What the fuck is going on?" She shouts into the phone. "You promised me that—"

"Hey, stop - this wasn't me. My brother and Celso came to an agreement in order to get funding for his stupid campaign." I blurt out defensively.

"Celso and your brother - Luke agreed to this?"

"Luke *planned this whole thing.*" I say tensely.

"I'll kill him. I'll kill them both. I'll speak to my father. I'll have him put an end to this. I won't let this happen."

"Dalila - stop - breathe. You sound like you're having a panic attack."

"I *am having a panic attack.*" She hisses.

"Breathe." I tell her again and hear her take a sharp, shallow breath.

"We can find a way out of this, ok. It only happened today. We have time to fix it."

"I don't know if we do. My brother is already making plans." She whimpers.

"Can you speak to your father?" I ask, hopefully.

"Yes. I'll go see him first thing in the morning. I'll fix it."

I nod, biting at the inside of my cheek. "Ok. Everything's going to be fine." I say, more to myself than her.

"Yeah." She agrees.

After a tense moment of silence, we say goodbye because I don't know what to say to her and she's too upset to speak.

She's my best friend. Yes, I've thought about being with Celso way more often than I should have been thinking about it, but I wouldn't have actually done it. I wouldn't have risked losing her over this.

I sigh, shoving the pillow over my face.

He's on this wild mission to marry me and I think it's freaking hormones. Maybe if I had slept with him, he would have seen that I'm a normal girl - nothing special - and he would've gotten over his obsession. Guys only want what they can't have. That's what this comes down to. He wants me because I'm forbidden, out of reach, something he was never allowed.

After the wedding he will get bored with me and start ignoring me and my life will suck.

Whatever fantasy I have of him being in love with me, like really in love - that's all it is. A fantasy. I'm not naive.

But as I lie there alone on my bed my hand drifts down my body, slipping beneath the waistline of my sweatpants.

Celso pushes my bedroom door open, walking in uninvited.

"Can't wait until the wedding night, my angel. I want you now." He growls.

I sit up in my bed, horrified to see him. "No, I don't even want to marry you - get out of my room." I shouted.

He laughs, that smooth, carefree sound that sends ripples through me. "I always get what I want, angel. Haven't you figured that out yet?"

I move to stand up and he shoves me back down, my back landing on my bed as he pins me down with his solid, muscular body. He is so much bigger than me, no matter how hard I resist him it's no use. I don't stand a chance against him.

He grabs my wrists and pins them above my head, snarling at me to behave as he pushes my legs wide open, my skirt bunching up over my hips.

"Stop" I say, breathless and flooded with desire.

He kisses me to silence my words, his lips pressed over mine as his cock rubs over my pussy.

"Please, stop." I beg him as he slams his cock into me.

The sudden sensation of being filled by his massive, throbbing cock is a complete shock to my body.

I shudder and tilt my head back, my eyes fluttering closed.

"I knew you would love it." He growls against my ear as he pulls back and slams into me again.

I cry out in desperation and pleasure.

"Stop." I mutter, but it's barely a whisper and if he tried to stop now, I wouldn't let him.

"Don't you see how you make me lose control, Neve. I can't be without you. You are the only thing I've ever wanted." He snarls, his cock thrusting even deeper than before. My pussy throbbing over him, my entire body melting against him.

"You belong to me." He whispers.

My entire body goes rigid as the orgasm pulses through me. Wave after wave of blissful release. I take a deep breath, my lips parted, my heart beating fast.

I'm hot, and my cheeks flush bright red with embarrassment.

It's not the first time I've done that while thinking of Celso. But now I know it might really happen - it feels even more wrong of me to want it.

CHAPTER SIXTEEN
Celso

I'm moving fast with all the arrangements because I don't want to risk this not happening. I won't allow it to fall through. Dalila has already tried to sabotage my agreement with Luke by involving my father, he was angry when he found out what I'd done. He told me I had no right to ask favors of the politician he owned. I told him the politician he owned was dead and I now own that man's son.

He was not impressed and continued to tell me I had to cancel the wedding.

But I only had to ask one question to get my father to back off with his anger.

He stood glaring at me, and I looked up from the sofa, calm and confident. I asked him, "Did you kill my mother?"

The question was like a punch to the face.

I could see it in his eyes.

The truth was so fucking clear, and he knew it. It was obvious.

"No - I - where did you hear that?"

I didn't answer him. I stood up, dusted my hand over my shoulder and said, "The wedding is on Saturday. Best you get your tuxedo ready and act the part."

He didn't say a word when I walked out - and he hasn't said a word to me since.

Dalila is furious. She has been calling me non-stop, demanding I don't do this.

But, honestly, it's all background noise.

Today, Neve moved into my place. The wedding is in two days, and I want her here, with me, to avoid any issues. She's been staying in her father's house with her brother, and I know they aren't getting along at the moment - for obvious reasons

- so I requested to have her things collected and brought here.

Her brother made the arrangements, and Neve was caught off guard when she got home and was told she didn't live there anymore.

Now she is upstairs in our bedroom, refusing to speak to me. With only one more day before our wedding I hope she can pull through and play her part.

I climb the stairs holding her plate of food in my hand.

Pushing our bedroom door open, I walk inside without knocking or saying anything.

She huffs, her back towards me, lying on her side on the bed.

"Neve, I brought you some early dinner before we have to get going."

"I'm not hungry. And I don't want to be here." She snaps.

"Well, you are going to eat, and you have to be here, so embrace it and let's move on from this attitude you're giving me." I snap back at her.

She doesn't reply.

Sitting on the edge of the bed I set her plate down on the side table and reach out to touch her. She shifts away from me, so I grab her leg and pull her back close to me.

"The news is being announced tonight. We are making a public appearance at an art gallery opening. You will be on your best behavior." I warned her.

She lifts her eyes towards me.

"And if I'm not?" She asks, heated with defiance.

I tug her further down the bed and move quickly. In a flash I am lying with my body on top of hers, pinning her down. Her breath is hot against my face when she cries out in fright. "If you do not behave, I will have to punish you." I say, running my hand up her thigh and over her waist.

She shudders beneath my touch and her eyes flood with lust.

I chuckle and climb off her.

Fuck. I want her so badly, but I'm willing to wait

until she belongs to me. I'm willing to wait until our wedding night to make it special.

"I hate you." She mutters, flushing with embarrassment at her own desire.

"Well, eat something while you hate me. And then put on that dress." I gesture towards the gold dress hanging on the outside of the closet. "We are leaving in one hour."

"I don't want to be married, Celso." She pleads. "This isn't what I want for my life. I'm so tired of other people controlling me and telling me what I have to do." Tears spill over the edge of her gorgeous blue eyes and my heart tightens.

"Marriage to me will not be what you think it is, Neve. You can still have everything you want for your life - we'll do it all together."

"You don't want the same things as me." She mumbles.

I reach out and touch her face. "What do you want, my angel?"

"I want—" She's flustered, agitated, heated "I want to travel. But not that luxury bull shit with five-star hotels. I want to see jungles and temples and climb those massive ruins in Peru. I want to learn to fly a helicopter and to learn how to scuba dive. I want to see the world - I don't want to be stuck - I don't want to be some well-behaved wife sitting neatly in her chair, smiling for the camera." Her voice trails off.

"Don't underestimate what I can give you, Neve." I say, letting my fingers trace over her thigh for a moment before I stand up. "Get ready." I say and leave her to make her own choices. But if she isn't ready in an hour, there will be hell to pay, and she knows it.

Besides, as much as she hates her brother right now - she doesn't want him out on the streets, homeless and ashamed. And I am the only one who can help him.

Neve comes downstairs, walking slowly and carefully in her stilettos and that gorgeous gold dress. It flows over her body like the ocean caressing the sandy shores of some tropical island.

"Fuck." I mutter, wondering how I am supposed to wait when she looks like that.

Neve huffs and rolls her eyes at me. "Let's go." She snaps, pushing past me.

I chuckle and follow her out to the car. The driver opens the door for her, and we both climb into the back seat.

"Let's get this over with." She says, shifting away from me.

She will learn, no matter what it takes. I grab her around the waist and tug her right back next to me.

"You are my fiancé, Neve. Act like it." I warn her.

She bites her lip and stops herself from saying whatever she was going to sass back at me.

The gallery opening is perfect. Photographers flock around us, snapping photos of Neve leaning against my body, her hand resting on my chest as she glances at the camera over her shoulder with the most gorgeous smile on her face.

She is brilliant. She has them eating out of her hand. She has me almost believing that she's accepted that she is going to be my wife.

She leans close and whispers in my ear, letting the camera's catch intimate moments that aren't even real. Her words, "Don't get used to this."

I grin. "I'm already used to this, angel." I laugh, tightening my hand against her lower back and pushing her hips against mine.

She smirks with an arrogant flare of defiance, but the playful darkness in her eyes betrays her. She can't wait to have my cock inside her. She's begging me with those blue eyes. Her plump pink lips pout towards me.

I lean down and wrap my hand around the back of her head and kiss her.

She is mine.

Let all the world see it.

Camera's fire and more photographs seal our fate.

Tomorrow is the last day she has left. After that - come hell fire or atomic blasts - she is mine. She will have my name, she will endure the heat of my desire, she will belong to me.

And that is how it will be until the day I die.

Neve moves through the evening in perfection. Laughing at jokes, gushing over me, pretending to be madly and wildly in love.

But the moment we arrive home, and the front door slams shut behind us - she turns.

Her sweetness turns cold and cruel. She kicks off her shoes and when I bend down to pick them up for her and to follow her up to bed, she glares at me.

"That was horrible." She mutters.

"No, it wasn't. Don't lie to me, angel." I sigh in frustration. "I saw you were having fun."

"Fun? With a million cameras in my face?" She flusters.

"No - *fun spending time with me.*"

She opens her mouth to say something and then slams her lips closed again.

I step closer to her, backing her up against the wall. "Don't fuck with me, Neve. I know you. I know your moods. I know your expressions. I know everything about you."

"Oh, please." She tries to argue.

"I know you are so fucking wet right now your body is screaming for me to fuck you."

I wrap my hand around her throat.

"Fuck off." She says.

"Are you denying it?" I whisper against her lips.

"Leave me alone. I don't want you."

I pull the slit of her gold dress to the side and run my hand up the inside of her thigh.

"We can check - I can prove it to you right now." I growl.

Neve gasps and shivers beneath my touch. Her pupils dilate and it's all I need to see to prove my point.

If I touch her now, if I dip my fingers inside her - I won't be able to stop. Already my cock is trying to rip through my pants.

"Good night, my angel. There is only one more day you have to wait - and then you can have all of me. I promise you - you will love every fucking second of it." I step away from her and she takes a sharp breath.

I chuckle again and her eyes flare. Her skin flushed pink.

The only reason it's possible to walk away from her and that tight, gorgeous little body of hers is because I am confident in my knowledge that the right time is coming soon.

I fall asleep easily, drift off with a smile on my face.

During the night I wake up to find that Neve never came to bed. Her side of the bed is unwrinkled. Instantly, rage floods me. Did she leave? Did she run away in the night? I leap out of bed and storm downstairs.

But she's sound asleep on the sofa in the living room. A small blanket was wrapped over her, still wearing the gold dress.

I lift her from the sofa, holding her cradled against my chest as I carry her up to our bedroom. I won't allow her to do that. She is going to be my wife, and she will share my bed.

I set her down on the bed and gently unzip the side of her dress, pulling it off her shoulders. Shifting her I pull it down her body while she mutters in her sleep. My cock is throbbing again. Her body is perfection.

How can I wait until tomorrow when she is lying on my bed in nothing but a pair of black lace panties?

I quickly throw the blankets over her and clench my jaw until my face aches.

I will wait.

Climbing into bed I move close to her, wrapping my arm around her naked body and pulling her right up against me. My cock throbs pressed against her ass.

I will wait.

She moves in her sleep, snuggling closer to me, her ass pushing harder against my cock.

It is going to be so fucking incredible. The moment I thrust into her.

My wife.

I close my eyes and force myself to go back to sleep.

CHAPTER SEVENTEEN
Neve

On the morning of our wedding, I'm still in denial that any of this is real.

Dalila is here with me, in my hotel room while makeup artists and hairdressers' fuss around me.

"I can't believe this is happening again." I sigh in frustration.

"I can't believe it either. It's so fucked up." She huffs, sitting next to me, also getting her hair done.

"Dalila, please don't let this ruin our friendship." I glance at her reflection in the mirror. Our eyes meeting in the silver sheet of glass.

She bites her lip, rolls her eyes and shrugs. "It's not you I'm angry with. It's my brother."

"So - you don't hate me?" I ask tensely.

She laughs. "No. Dumbass."

I reach out and take her hand, squeezing it, smiling at her. "I am so happy you are here with me - again. I need you today."

"I'm glad I can be here for you, babe. I wish my father had listened to me."

And I wish I could be more honest with my friend.

I wish I could tell her I'm less nervous about today's wedding, about marrying her brother, than I was about marrying Damion. I wish I could tell her I'm a little bit excited, even though I'm angry, I'm looking forward to seeing where this leads.

But I can't tell her that - and a huge part of the reason I can't tell her is that I can't admit it to myself yet.

I'm still aggressively denying my attraction to him, even though I can't keep my eyes off him when he's near me. The things he's been doing to me.

Undressing me and lying with his body pressed against mine - his forceful nature - the darkness in his eyes. It's all driving me crazy with desire. I want him. I don't want to want him, but I have to have him.

It's so complicated.

And in a few hours, we are going to be married.

"At least the groom is here." Dalila chuckles, and her mouth drops open in horror. "Oh, my word, Neve, I'm so sorry that was a terrible joke. I can't believe I said that I have absolutely no filter on my brain sometimes—"

I giggle. She pauses, pressing her lips closed. Then she laughs too.

"You're not wrong." I laugh even harder and the makeup artists sighs.

"Oh *whatever*, it's my wedding I can do whatever I want." I snap at her.

She straightens her shoulders and nods. "Yes, no, I didn't mean—"

Dalila laughs again, and it sets me off.

After a good five minutes of laughing, I feel so much better.

It's an incredible way to get rid of tension.

With our makeup done all we need to do is put our dresses on. Dalila in a pastel blue bridesmaid dress that looks magnificent on her - and me in a wedding dress that Celso chose for me. And to my surprise it's perfect. I love it. He gave me three options, they all got delivered to my hotel room early this morning, but this is the one that screamed my name.

It has thin spaghetti straps, and a low dipped front, showing off some cleavage. The back dips even lower than the front though showing off my back all the way down to the curve right before my butt. It's comfortable, elegant, timeless, and it makes me feel like a princess.

I can breathe in it, which was the most important thing for me. I grin as I slip it up over my body and adjust the straps. Looking in the mirror at myself with Dalila standing behind me, I have a moment where I am happy.

I'm calm and excited and - happy. Which is so unexpected.

"You are so beautiful I think I'm going to cry." She mumbles.

"Don't the makeup artist already left." I giggle.

"Ok. I'm going to go check on everything and see if they're ready. You take a moment alone and - do whatever - I won't be long.

She hurries out of the room. But almost as soon as the door closes, I hear it open again.

"What did you forget?" I giggle, turning towards her.

But it's Celso.

He is staring at me with his mouth open and his eyes wide with shock.

"You can't be in here." I stammer. "It's not allowed - it's against the rules or bad luck or something—"

He walks towards me, reaching out and touching my face. His black tuxedo, with a blue flower tucked into his pocket - his dark hair slicked back and his eyes looking clear and sharp - I can't stop staring at him. He's so freaking gorgeous.

"You are a goddess, Neve. My angel. Truly."

"Celso." I stammer, still horrified to see him in my room before we are supposed to get married.

He laughs.

"My sweet, innocent angel - fuck the rules and fuck bad luck. We make our own."

I narrow my eyes at him. *Fuck the rules.* I like the sound of that.

He reaches into his pocket and pulls out a velvet black box.

"I wanted to give you these." He said, taking one earring out.

Tear drop earrings in blue sapphire. They are stunning.

"You got these - for me?" I ask.

"They were my mothers. They are the only thing I have from her."

"Celso." I whisper, shocked that he would give them to me.

He removes the little diamond stud I am wearing and puts the tear drop sapphire earrings in for me. He turns me so that I can see myself in the mirror.

"Something blue." He whispers against my ear, his hand brushing over my stomach and my body sparking with wildfire.

When I look in the mirror, I see us standing together. We look like we belong. Like this is how it's supposed to be.

I swallow hard.

He leans down and kisses my neck.

"I'll see you in a few moments, my angel." He says, his breath warm on my skin.

And then he's gone.

For a moment I'm in shock, my skin still tingling. I reach up and touch the earrings, letting them dangle against my fingertips. They are so beautiful. It's so special.

Dalila comes bursting back into the room.

"It's time." She says.

And so, the chaos begins.

A wild, busy, noisy day filled with family, reporters, friends, strangers, promises, food, champagne - and all the while I'm trying to keep up with myself.

I'm fighting myself at every corner. I shouldn't be enjoying it. I should be barely tolerating his hands against me. But everything seems so wonderful.

I could pretend I chose him. I could pretend I am in love.

When we exchange our vows, his gaze is so tender as he says the words, promising me he will always love me.

When the priest says, "I now pronounce you husband and wife." My heart does a somersault, and my entire body spins when Celso dips me backwards to kiss me in front of a thousand people.

To me it seems like everything happened in a wild blur.

"Dance with me." He says, the after party is loud and people are tipsy. I'm one of those people. I've had too much champagne and I'm having proper fun now.

But in the back of my mind, I know what Celso wants when we get home and I'm terrified that I might want it too.

He leads me onto the dance floor and holds me right up against his body.

We move together, the champagne giving me courage I should not have.

"You look incredible, my love. My *wife*." He grins.

I bite my lip, not sure how to respond. He speaks to me as though he loves me.

"Tonight was everything I dreamed it would be." He nuzzles his face against my neck and my body tingles with delight. "And when we get to the honeymoon suite, it will be even more perfect."

Fighting my arousal, still trying to deny it, I push away from him. But he won't let me. He tugs me close again and darkness flares in his eyes.

"Are we still playing games, Neve?" His voice is low and filled with warning.

"You don't get to take what you want." I say back, smirking with attitude.

"I have already taken what I want. And tonight, I will take everything else that belongs to me." He says.

"Hmm." I huff, acting disinterested. I see his eyes flare again. It shoots through me like an electric current.

"I think the party is over." He says.

"It's not even midnight." I complain.

"We are done here." He commands and blood pulses faster through my veins.

He takes my hand and leads me out of the venue, straight into the elevators.

As soon as though elevators close, he shoves me against the wall and kisses me.

I bite down hard on his lip, tasting blood. I shove him back, just as hard. His lips curl upwards and the smile on his face is tainted with a darkness so deep it terrifies me - but it also sets a fire between my legs.

"Angel." He warns me. "I will have what I want."

"No. You won't." I taunt him, biting my lip. "You make these promises, but I image you can't keep half of them." I sass.

The elevator opens on our floor, and he scoops me into his arms and carries me towards the honeymoon suite. I squeal and wiggle, but his grip is tight.

He kicks the door closed behind us and sets me down. As soon as my feet hit the ground, I make a run for it.

But Celso is faster, grabbing me around the waist and throwing me onto the sofa.

I squeal again and roll over to face him. He tugs his jacket off, tossing it aside.

He pounces on me like a wild animal.

His fingers lock around my throat as he pushes my dress up over my thighs.

I kick and grab at his hands, but he is so much stronger than me. In the fight I rip his shirt open and buttons scatter around us. His muscles ripple when he moves, pushing his cock against my pussy to tease me.

A soft, reluctant moan of pleasure escapes my lips and my cheeks flush pink. I can feel the heat of my embarrassment. I'm so turned on by him - and I can't even try to hide it.

He chuckles as he stares down at me, looming over me like a perfectly sculpted giant.

He stands up and pulls me with him, his lips crashing into mine.

While he kisses me, he is pulling at my wedding dress. I still want to fight him. Even though I am so fucking turned on, I want to keep fighting.

I push his hands away, turn my head to the side - doing everything I can to make it difficult for him.

My dress falls to the floor around my feet, and he sees the white lingerie I'm wearing.

He growls and bites his lip.

"You fucking want this—" he smirks, while his eyes eat me alive. "You would never have put this one on if you didn't want this." He slips his finger beneath the sheer white lace of my bra, and it brushes over my nipple. Sharp electric spikes of pleasure shoot through me.

I turn to run. But again, he is too quick.

My heart is beating so hard I can barely breathe.

Celso grabs a handful of my hair and shoves me

back down onto the sofa, my ass in the air, pointed right at him while my face is buried in the pillows.

I scream as he pushes my face down, and he chuckles. "Are you having fun yet?" he asks, tugging his belt off.

He lets the leather belt brush over my ass cheek. "You're lucky I don't use this on you, angel." I wiggle my ass, trying to free myself from his grip, but his cock brushes over my ass cheek, and I freeze. He stands up, leans forward again and his fingers slip beneath the delicate lace and in an instant, he has ripped my panties off my body.

My pussy is throbbing and pulsing and dripping with need. I am shocked by how turned on I am.

The desire pulsing in my body is almost feverish, making me dizzy and desperate.

A soft whimper escapes my lips, giving away my wish.

I want him to fuck me.

I want him to fuck me like he is claiming me as his own. Everything he has said, every time he's told me I belong to him - I want to feel it. I arch my back towards him, begging him.

His cock brushes between my legs, over my pussy, and I shudder with need.

CHAPTER EIGHTEEN
Celso

I have her pinned against the couch, unable to move. She's been fighting against me since the moment we got into that elevator and all its achieved is making me want her more.

My cock is so fucking hard right now I'm in pain.

But Neve can't hide her true feelings from me. She can't hide her desire or her body's response and right now, with my cock pressed between her ass cheeks, she can't hide how wet her pussy is and how she's arching her ass up towards me. I chuckle. A low deep sound that vibrates through the air.

I have what I want, right in front of me. I thought our first time together would be gentle, possibly romantic. But she clearly didn't want that - and now I don't either.

I want to fuck her how I've fucked her in my dreams.

Bent over the sofa, locked in my grip, unable to escape while I claim her with every thrust of my cock.

I grab my cock in my hand and let the tip slide over her pussy.

"Oh fuck." She whimpers, her voice muffled against the pillows.

"Beg me to fuck you, angel. Beg for it."

"I won't." She screams, kicking back and trying to get away again.

I laugh louder. "The harder you fight - the harder my cock gets." I warn her as it throbs in my hand, pulsing with desire to be inside my wife.

"I've told you, Neve. You belong to me."

"I will never—"

I thrust my cock into her pussy so hard she can't speak. I push so deep inside her my cock is buried all the way into her, penetrating her and claiming her in the most intimate way.

"You are mine." I growl, rocking backwards and slamming into her again.

She cries out and her fingers knot around the fabric of the pillows. She rocks her body backwards against me.

I have never felt such intense pleasure in my life. And I don't want it to end.

But I can't control myself as I fuck her harder and faster, my cock spreading her tight little pussy wide open, filling her up, moving inside her and making her scream.

Her legs begin to shake, and I smirk. She's going to come before I am. She's loving every second of this.

I keep pushing forward until her pussy starts to tighten around me.

I pull out.

Neve cries out in horror.

I step back, my cock standing erect, solid with thick veins throbbing along the shaft.

She stands up and turns to stare at me with wide eyes.

I sit down on the sofa.

"Sit on my cock." I demand.

She bites her lip, looking down at me.

"Spread your legs over me and sit on my cock, Neve." I demand again.

She hesitates so I grab her arm and pull her forward, spreading her legs over my lap so that she can straddle me.

Her breathing is heavy and fast, and her lips are swollen with desire.

I take her hips and shove her onto my cock.

She cries out, grabbing my shoulders.

Lifting her and slamming her back down onto my lap I use her to fuck me.

Growling with pleasure as her breasts bounce in front of my face, I keep pushing her up and down on my cock until she is shaking, and tears are streaming down her cheeks.

Her body lets go as her pupils dilate and she tilts her head backwards. I can't hold out much longer. This is too perfect.

The orgasm hits her like a tidal wave. Her pussy tightens over my cock and wave after wave of muscular contractions have her body convulsing and soft moans of delight falling from her lips.

I slam her down onto my cock one last time and hold her there as I explode inside her, my pleasure flooding from me in pure ecstasy.

Neve sits on my cock, gasping for breath, staring at me with shock in her eyes.

"Mrs. Vece." I mutter, admiring my wife, in all of her perfection.

I lift her off my lap, standing as I do so and wrapping her legs around my waist.

Carrying her to the bedroom I let her feet drop to the floor.

She stands in front of me, in some kind of trance, still shocked from how good we are together. "I promised you, didn't I?" I say. She nods, licking her lips.

I begin to undress her, unclipping the gorgeous white lingerie and letting each piece fall to the floor until she is naked.

I carry her to the shower and stand with her as I wash her body, touching every part of her.

The first time - we *fucked*, but the second time in the shower, we make love. It's slower, tender, more intimate as she wraps her legs around my waist, and I fuck her against the wall with hot water splashing over us.

We fall asleep wrapped in each other's arms and for the first time I think Neve is letting me in.

She's softened to me and allowing me to love her in the way that I want to love her.

I wake up before her.

It's a little chilly because the sun isn't up yet. Neve is curled against me, her hair tickling my face. I smile, taking in a quiet breath of her scent. This is what I've waited so long for. I can't believe I finally have this gorgeous creature here in my arms in the quietest hours of the morning - and she is my wife.

My arms are already wrapped around her, her back fitting perfectly against my chest. I pull her a little closer and close my eyes again.

I'm not rushing to get out of bed today. I have all the time in the world to lie here with her. This is exactly where I want to be.

I fall asleep again. Content. So comfortable I don't even dream, or at least not that I remember. When I realize I haven't had a single nightmare since Neve has been sleeping next to me. She is the cure to everything bad in my life.

When I wake up the second time, she is already out of bed, and I groan in annoyance.

Why didn't she stay with me, snuggle with me?

I throw the blankets aside and swing my legs off the edge of the bed, stretching my sleepy body until it wakes up.

Heading downstairs to the kitchen, I assume I'll find her there because I can smell fresh coffee.

She's leaning over the coffee machine, muttering in annoyance. The t-shirt she threw on to come downstairs is barely covering her ass. The sight of her leaning forward like that makes my cock stir and my body light with desire.

She is my wife.

Perhaps I should take her again, over the kitchen counter. We could have fun in every room of this hotel before we leave for our home - then we could do it all again there.

She mutters again and huffs at the coffee machine.

I grin. Oddly, it's the same machine we have at home.

And she keeps forgetting it's the silver button on the side that does all in one option. Every time she uses our machine, she pushes the first one and gets a black coffee. She's done the same thing here.

Slipping my hands around her waist I whisper against her ear. "Good morning, my love."

She jumps, already agitated from her coffee machine issues.

"Don't do that." She snaps a little and pulls her mouth to the side and narrows her eyes at me. "It's just me - the man you married last night." I smirk.

She glares and I stare back intensely. The looks she gives me says several things. The most obvious one is that she has changed her mood since last night's intimacy. We might be leaning back towards the 'don't touch me, I don't want to be here' phase.

I decided to ignore it.

I tug her against my chest and kiss the top of her head.

She wiggles a little, brushing her body against me. My cock goes hard, and her eyes widen.

"Did you sleep well, my angel?" I ask, reaching around her and putting a fresh cup under the machine and pushing the button on the side.

"Dammit. I *always* forget." She sighs, seeing which one I pressed. "Like, how hard can a freaking coffee machine be?" she rolls her eyes at herself.

"Did you?" I ask again. Looking down at her, my arms still wrapped around her even though she hasn't hugged me back. She pulls her mouth to the side. "Sure. Yes. I slept very well." She admits as though I'm interrogating her.

I take her arms and wrap them around my waist.

"This is how you greet your husband in the morning, angel." I grin.

She tries to hide the little giggle that rustles through her, but she doesn't manage to.

Wrapping my hands around her waist I lift her onto the kitchen counter, away from the coffee machine.

"Also, you are supposed to stay in bed so that I can make you coffee in the morning and kiss you awake with a fresh cup." I say. "What is this nonsense where you get up before me and I wake up alone?" I hand her the coffee and she sips it.

She bites her lip to hide her smile.

"If I waited for you to get up, I'd be sleeping all day. I don't have time for that." She sasses.

"Is that so?" I step close to her, pushing her legs open and taking her face in my hand to kiss her. I can taste the sweetness of coffee on her lips.

"What would you like to do today, my angel?" I ask, mesmerized by her eyes.

"Um - escape a forced marriage and maybe disappear in Mexico so my crazy husband can't find me." She replies, her brows raised.

"Oh, sweet little angel, your crazy husband would tear every continent apart to find you. If I had to kill every person on this planet until you were the last one alive - just to find you - that is what I would do." I say. A promise she doesn't know I would keep.

She stiffens a little, her fingers tight around the coffee mug. Perhaps she understands a little about how far I would go to have her.

I smile as I watch her. Tracing my fingers over her jaw, I let the pad of my thumb brush across her lips.

"Don't test me, my angel." I warn her.

She nods, ever so slightly, almost unnoticeable.

Except I notice everything.

CHAPTER NINETEEN
Neve

I woke up a little freaked out.

Celso had his arms around me and to be entirely and utterly honest with myself - it felt amazing. It was like we fit together perfectly. And don't even get me started on last night.

What the hell was that?

How was it so fucking good?

How is it possible for a man to make me feel that incredible?

I was lying there snuggled against Celso and suddenly I felt too comfortable, too happy - and yes - it freaked me out.

So, I wiggled out of bed without waking him up. I grabbed a T-shirt and hurried down to the kitchen. For a while all I could do is stand there in shock over last night's experience and how quickly he is winning me over.

I shouldn't be this easy.

But then I wanted coffee - and because the universe likes to test me at every chance, it can get - the coffee machine is identical to the one Celso has in his home. *Our home.*

And I pushed the wrong button.

Now, Celso is standing with his hips pushed between my legs, his thumb brushing over my lips and my heart is racing at the sight of him.

I'm trying so hard not to make this easy for him, but I can't help the way he makes me feel.

"Don't test me, my angel." He whispers, a darkness touching his words.

It sends a current of fear and desire washing over me. I nod.

I want him again.

Last night was the most incredible experience. The way he took me, I felt - *free*.

Celso chuckles and he's close enough to me his chest vibrates and my body tingles. I want to wrap my arms around him and pull him even closer. I want to trace my tongue over the muscles on his stomach. I want to taste him.

But I also want to let him know he doesn't own me. And he seems to think he does.

With a cheeky smile on my face, I decide to choose to do something today that is the most unlikely thing a man like Celso would enjoy. I'm determined to annoy him.

"I would like to go to the natural goods market in the park." I love markets.

I watch his face, waiting for the glimmer of annoyance or disappointment, but one side of his mouth curves upward into that gorgeous smile, pressing a dimple into his cheek - and he says, "That sounds perfect. We can have breakfast there. They have the best homemade foods at those things."

It takes me by surprise. I try to hide it, but I think he notices my eyes flare open.

His grin widens and my heart beats a little faster.

"I'm ready when you are." He says.

"You're going in your sweatpants and nothing else?" I giggle.

"And you can go in nothing but that t-shirt. We would cause quite a scene. But I told you - we make our own rules, Neve."

Walking around the market, Celso always wants to touch me. He will hold my hand or keep his hand resting on my lower back. He will wrap his arm around me and kiss the top of my head while I browse some of the market stalls. He holds me close and makes me feel so wanted it's almost impossible not to fall a little deeper for him.

In all honesty I don't even think I'm fighting it anymore.

Between the incredible chemistry we obviously share and his ridiculously tender way of handling me - and his obvious obsession with me - I have never been so desired and so adored.

Of course, in the back of my mind I'm waiting for him to get bored with me. For the spark to wear off and for reality to kick in. It's how the real world works, unfortunately. The fairytale of who you think someone is fade away when you finally get them.

He'll wake up soon and be bored with me and he'll find a new girl to obsess over, and I'll be the wife he keeps at home because he is obliged to.

But right now, walking around a random Sunday afternoon market, I laugh with him, leaning towards him, enjoying the warmth and connection. I can let myself enjoy this for a little while. I have to be careful with my heart.

Celso grabs my hand. "Neve, you'll love these." He says a spark of excitement in his eyes. He pulls me towards one stall and sets me in front of his body so that I can see what he's spotted.

My heart melts.

I don't know what I was expecting, but I didn't expect him to know things like this about me.

I stand there, staring at the dark chocolate color leather boots. They are army style, a little rugged looking, but still feminine and cute if paired with the right outfit.

"Oh." I say, my voice tight. "What makes you think I'll like these?" I ask, curious to see if it's a wild guess he's making, because he's spot on. I freaking love them.

"Aren't they perfect for the adventure we are going to go on - hiking through the jungles of Peru? Searching for ruins and lost temples?"

I glance over my shoulder, looking up at him with my brows knotted.

"You remembered?"

"Of course, I remembered." He says, knotting his brows too, confused why I thought, for even a moment that he wouldn't remember.

I turn back to the boots, but my mind is muddled. Why is he so sweet and tender? How is it he listens and knows things about me that my family didn't bother to know?

"What color do you want?" Celso asks, pointing out the black, caramel, and dark chocolate options.

"Um, what do you think?" I ask, unsure, still taken by surprise.

"It's hard to choose, but I can picture you in these and some cute little shorts, or a summer dress. Us on a road trip, your feet up on the dashboard - maybe we need to get two. I'd say black and caramel?"

I nod, picturing us on that road trip and thinking it is the most perfect thing he could have said. An image of freedom, the wind in my hair as we drive through a desert somewhere - lost together.

Celso buys two pairs of those boots for me and carries the paper shopping bag, filling it up with other things he buys me, as we roam the rest of the market. We get home-made custard pies and coffee, and Chinese noodles for lunch when we feel like taking a break, and we sit on the grass, letting the sun warm our faces. Celso pulls me close to him so that I can lean my back against his chest while we watch other people walking past.

It's late when we return to the hotel and pack up our things to go home.

And I'm happy.

I haven't been happy in so long it's a weird thing for me to accept. Especially that I am happy with a man like Celso. With the man who I was terrified of. He is warm, generous, buying everything that makes me smile - he is attentive and affectionate.

He whispers in my ear that he thinks I am beautiful. He kisses my face and plays with my hair.

How can I not fall for him?

Over the next week things only seem to get better, and it takes everything in me to stay cautiously aware that at any moment he might get bored with me and drop me like a stone into a deep, deep lake.

"I ordered Chinese." He calls upstairs. I'm climbing out of the shower, a thick fluffy towel wrapped around me and a smaller one wrapped around my hair. "I'll be down in a second." I call back, but he walks into the room and wraps me in his arms. "Hi gorgeous, I missed you." He grins and presses his lips against mine.

"You were only gone for a few hours." I giggle as he scatters kisses across the rest of my face.

"Mm. A few hours too long. But I saw something, and it instantly made me think of you."

"What was it?" I ask, curious.

"Come downstairs and find out. I'll get the plates out for dinner. Wear something cozy. We can watch a movie after dinner and snuggle on the sofa." He kisses me again, steps back, admiring me for a moment before he grins and leaves the room.

Even these small interactions make my heart flutter and widen the smile on my lips. He keeps me curious, and his affection keeps me wanting more.

I get dressed in a hurry, wanting to know what he saw.

Wearing my comfy sweatpants and a little crop top I skip down the stairs like a child on Christmas morning.

When I walk into the living room where he has spread assorted Chinese takeouts on the coffee table - I burst out laughing.

There is a life-sized llama teddy bear standing next to the sofa.

I can't stop laughing at the randomness of it.

"A llama?" I ask through my giggles.

"Not any llama." He grins, walking over to it with his hands behind his back.

He sets a tiny sombrero on its head. "It's a Mexican llama."

I shake my head and scrunch my nose. "Why is there a Mexican llama in our living room?" I ask, walking towards it and running my fingers through its fluffy teddy bear coating.

He wraps his arm around my waist and holds me against his body, whispering in my ear.

"Because he's going to help us plan for our honeymoon."

I scrunch my nose again. "Our honeymoon? I thought—"

"You thought we weren't going on one?" he asks in horror. "Neve, the wedding was crazy - rushed - and I have some things I need to close off at work before we can leave, but I am definitely taking you on a honeymoon. An adventure of your dreams. I thought we should go to Peru and because it's almost October, we can time our trip so that we are in Mexico right during the Día de los Muertos festival."

"Day of the dead." I whisper. "That festival has always been something I wanted to see." For a second, I'm fighting tears. This is all so overwhelming.

"I want to see that festival too - but only with you, my angel." He says, his lips brushing against my cheek. I turn in his arms and lift my face towards his. I pull him close and kiss him.

This is the first time I have initiated a kiss.

My heart screams with wild excitement and his cock goes hard.

I giggle because I am so happy to hold it inside me.

He steps away from me, chuckling and shaking his head.

"You will be the death of me, Neve." He laughs. "Let's eat before everything gets cold and after that I will do things to you that you can't even dream of." His eyes are dark and full of promise.

We both sit on the floor at the low coffee table and eat straight out of the boxes as we talk about the different things we want to see when we travel. It's not only Mexico we talk about. It's Asia too -

Cambodia and Vietnam - the gorgeous temples there and the lost jungle paths. Again, I can't stop smiling because I've never found someone who was as excited about these things as I am.

Why does he have to be so perfect?

CHAPTER TWENTY
Celso

It's been two weeks since our wedding and my life has never been more perfect.

Neve is everything I've ever wanted - and more. She is so much more.

Her smile lights my heart on fire. Her laughter sets my entire body alight.

I hate being away from her, and when I do have to leave, I rush home, excited to see her again.

I couldn't imagine my life being better than it is right now, but despite that - it seems to get better each day she opens up to me a little more.

She is waiting for it all to fall apart. I don't understand why she would think that, but I guess she does not know how hard I fought to get her. How many years I've waited to have her by my side. She's here now, she belongs to me, and I will never, ever let her go.

"Are you ready?" I ask, walking into the bedroom. Neve is doing the finishing touches to her hair, pulling a few strands free from her bun so that they can curl around her face. I lean against the doorframe and watch her. I love to watch her. Those tight jeans hug her ass and hips in the sexiest way and her little crop top shows off the right amount of skin to tease me.

She is wearing her leather boots, the caramel ones. The sweet tone of them matches her light hair.

"Are you breaking those boots in for our honeymoon?" I grin.

"It's so hard to get dressed when you don't tell me where we're going. I chose this." She waves her hands over her body. "But what if you're planning on taking me to a five-star restaurant and I look like a homeless person when I walk in there—"

She scrunches her nose at me. I love it when she does that.

"My love, you look like Miss Universe no matter what you wear. And I don't know how many times I have to tell you - you should wear whatever you are in the mood to wear no matter where we're going."

"Well - I was in the mood to break my boots in a little, so they are more comfortable when we hike through the wild jungles of Peru."

I push myself off the doorframe and walk over to her. "And Cambodia." I grin, kissing her. I let my hand run down her back and over her ass. Squeezing her cheeks I lift her, and she wraps her legs around my waist. I kiss my wife in the way she deserves to be kissed. I kiss her to let her know how beautiful she is and that I would do anything for her.

When I set her down again her cheeks are rosy and pink, and her lips are plumper than they were before. She smiles and narrows her eyes at me. "Where are we going?" She asks, reaching up and brushing her fingers over my jaw. Her tender, quiet touch makes me want to throw her onto the bed and cancel all our plans. It makes my heart overheat and my body alive with desire.

"You'll find out soon enough."

The drive doesn't take us long.

I've booked the top of the tallest building in the city. There is a telescope, a glass dome, and a lookout point. Beneath the glass dome I've had them set up a table for a private dinner and we can spend our evening up there watching the stars, looking across the ocean and being together.

I have decided that once a week for the rest of our lives I will come up with a romantic and unique date idea for us. Of course, every day I want to have a date with her. But some are quiet date nights at home. Some are afternoon dates, walking through the park and eating ice cream. Some are adventurous and some are calm. All of them are more special to me than any other time of the day when I'm not with her.

I want to make something as simple as going to the shops together a thing to enjoy. Life is short and once you've found the person, you can be obsessed with - you should never let a moment of your time with them be wasted. I savor every second I have with her - and I will for the rest of my life.

Neve looks unsteady when we get to the rooftop, and I guide her to the edge to see the view. She clings onto me a little tighter and I realize she's scared.

"You don't like heights?" I ask, worried I've made the wrong choice. "But how can you not like heights if you want to hike to the ruins and fly helicopters?"

She giggles, her face looking pale. She's terrified.

With her fingers gripped onto me she shakes her head. "No, you don't understand. Or you half do - um - I'm terrified of heights - but I love the idea of challenging myself to overcome it. Like right now, I know I'm safe, but the vertigo makes me dizzy, and my stomach is in such a knot I want to throw up."

"I'm so sorry." I say, wrapping my arms around her. "I didn't know. We can leave right now, and I'll take you somewhere else."

"Celso - this is amazing. This is perfect. I want to be up here. I might be a little jittery near the edge." She is grinning, looking proud of herself.

"You want to be a little scared?" I ask her, amused.

She nods, nudging closer to me.

"A lot of things make sense now." I chuckle.

"Why? Because challenging myself makes me happy?"

"No, because I think fear turns you on." I whisper.

In a moment of realization her lip's part and her eyes widen.

"That's not true—" She stammers. But I can feel her body, the heat against mine, the way she presses into me.

"It's true, my angel, and it's why we are so good together. And tonight, when the stars fill the sky, after sunset I am going to push you up against this railing and fuck you."

Her entire body shudders with pleasure as my words course through her.

I chuckle again and pull her away from the edge towards our table beneath the high arched glass dome. It's going to be an incredible night.

Early on Wednesday morning I get a call from Dalila. This surprises me because she hasn't spoken to me since the wedding. Even on the few times I've seen her in passing at my father's house - she wouldn't even look at me.

"Dalila." I answer cheerfully.

"Dad says you two should come for dinner on Tuesday night next week." She snaps.

"I'm happy you called."

"Listen, don't fuck with me, Celso. I'm still furious. I'm only phoning because dad made me phone you." She slams the phone down on me and I grin. Well. It's better than nothing at all. She really is angry though. I've never seen my sister so angry. And she's never gone this long without talking to me.

But I have a feeling that once Neve comes all the way around and accepts my love for what it is - when she relaxes and admits she wants this as much as I do - my sister will see that her friend is happy, and she'll come around too.

It'll take a little time, but I think I've already

proved to myself how patient I can be - and how wonderfully it pays off in the end.

The whole rule about not dating our sister's friends was only because she was scared it would frighten her friends away - after that incident when Dalila was in high school. But that's not how it is with Neve. This is forever. When they both see that things will change.

My sister and Neve hang out a lot. Or at least they did before the wedding. I'm tense when I realize that in the last two weeks they have spent no time together, and that is because of me. No wonder my sister sounds extra angry.

I head upstairs to the sunroom where Neve is reading in the early morning light, little dancing wisps of steam pour from her coffee into the fresh morning air.

"Dalila called to let us know about a family dinner next week." I say, walking towards her and standing alongside her chair, threading my fingers through her curls.

"Ok, it will be nice to see her." Neve says, her eyes wide and beautiful.

"Actually, I thought maybe you should spend the day with her, if you want to. Go shopping or for lunch or whatever you want to do. I know you two enjoy spending time together."

I hand her a credit card.

She takes it and stares at it. "What is this?"

"It's your card. It's linked to my account, there is no limit."

She looks uncomfortable for a moment, biting at her lip.

"Neve, you're my wife, that means I take care of every single thing you need or want."

"Thank you." she says, setting the card down on the side table next to her. "I would love to spend the day with Dalila. I'll call her now."

"Come have breakfast with me first though. I can make us crumpets with honey or salted caramel sauce."

"Mm. Caramel. *Salted* caramel."

"Done." I smile, brushing my hand under her chin and tilting her face towards me. I lean down and kiss her. "I'll miss you all day." I whisper against her lips.

After breakfast Neve gets dressed and Dalila comes to fetch her. I told her she can take any of my cars she wants to until she decides what car she wants for herself, but she said it was ridiculous for her to get her own car when I have five sitting in the garage. I didn't tell her about the others I have in the warehouse. Maybe I'll order her something as a surprise.

But today she was happy to have Dalila fetch her, and I think Dalila was over the moon to get the invite and was already driving her before Neve was even finished her breakfast.

I wave as they pull out of the parking area and Neve waves back while Dalila sticks her tongue out at me. So immature. I chuckle.

While Neve is out today, I am going to head over to the travel agent and get every brochure on Peru and Mexico that she has available. Neve and I can plan our adventure. Maybe I should get the Asia brochures too, in case she would prefer to go there. I want to give her all the options to make it the most perfect honeymoon imaginable.

Neve deserves the entire world - and I want to be the one who gives it to her.

CHAPTER TWENTY-ONE
Neve

I didn't realize how much I needed a girl's day out to clear my head.

Dalila arrives at the house around eleven in the morning and from the moment I climb into her car we are smiling and laughing.

Walking around the mall in the air-conditioned atmosphere, people hurrying back and forth around us while we browse clothing stores and look at handbags and shoes and accessories - I am thinking about how crazy the changes in my life have been and where I've landed up.

And the thing is - where I've landed up isn't bad at all.

"Celso is busy planning our honeymoon with me." I say, holding up a blue sweater to show Dalila.

"Mm. Maybe try the darker blue on, I think it might bring out your eyes more. So, where did you guys decide to go?" She asks, turning back to the rack of clothing she was browsing.

I pick up the darker blue cardigan, holding it up against my chest.

"He's been talking about Peru. Because I mentioned hiking Machu Picchu."

"That one looks great. Definitely that one. Machu Picchu - that sounds like your style of holiday. So, Celso isn't pushing for Hawaii or some luxurious tropical island?"

"No, he's going with what I want - and he seems to be excited about it too."

Dalila narrows her eyes and sighs.

"At the wedding I was watching him and I kind of have to admit - I don't think I've ever seen him smiling that much in my life. It was unnerving." She bursts out laughing.

"What do you mean *unnerving*?" I say in horror.

"It's *Celso*. He's always been serious and moody and broody. I don't know. It was weird to see him that happy."

I grin, my heart flickering. "Why do you think?"

"Obviously because he was getting to marry you, idiot." She answers me before I can finish my question.

I choose the blue sweater and a pair of bubblegum blue Nike hi-tops in almost the same color and carry them towards the checkout counter. Dalila has found a white summer dress and a pair of tan sneakers with a thick platform sole.

She glances at her watch while the lady rings up our items.

"Are you ready for a little lunch and a cocktail?" She asks. "Then we can do the other side of the mall after that and with two cocktails in us it'll be a much more reckless decision-making experience." The grin on her face is classic.

"Sounds perfect. I need to make some reckless fashion choices. I was always so perfectly groomed when my father sent me off shopping." I giggle.

Dalila leads us to her favorite sushi restaurant on the top floor of the mall. The wide glass walls overlook the shoppers down below us and we find a table near the edge so that we can watch the other people walking around.

"So, Mrs. Vece, how's life?" She teases me as sit down at the table we've chosen.

I go quiet as I contemplate her question because - while it is a normal question - it's thrown me off guard.

She scrunches her brows and looks at with her head tilted to the side. "What's going on?" she asks, worried.

The server arrives and right away Dalila orders two Mango and lime cocktails and a sushi platter, then chases him away.

She turns back to me, her forehead lined with worry. "Neve?" She says reaching out to touch my hand.

I giggle and shake my head. "Stop looking so worried." I laugh.

"Well, you went all quiet and weird and all I asked was how's life?"

"I got caught off guard." I shrug.

"By what?" she says confused.

"By my first thought when you asked it."

"Oh, for crying out loud will you tell me your answer?" she huffs, throwing her hands up.

I grin and shake my head again. "The very first answer that popped into my head was 'life's great.' But I had to pause for a second and think about it - because - well - my life hasn't been *great* before. It's been good. But controlled. Structured. Ruled. All those things - you know how my father was."

"Ok—" Dalila says, waiting for me to explain more as the server sets our drinks down on the table.

I take a long leisurely sip. It's lovely.

"Since I married Celso - ok, so in the beginning I was furious. But he isn't at all what I thought he was going to be. He lets me be who I am. I never feel judged - in fact, it's the complete opposite. I feel beautiful, and adored - I feel like he sees me—"

Dalila's face has relaxed, and she's looking at me with a trace of surprise in her bright green eyes.

"Are you *happy*, Neve?" She asks, confused.

"I am. I'm happy. How crazy is that?" I giggle, my cheeks turning warm pink as I confess something that I had not even realized yet. Not fully. Not enough to admit it out loud.

I take a deep breath. "Even my brother's campaign is soaring. He's doing so well. So, he's happy and my family name has been recovered after that disaster with my leaked photos of my father and his bullshit - and my brother doesn't seem to care about what I do. He is on his own mission, so he isn't trying to impose all this stupid rules on me like my father did. Celso is - he's amazing. I never expected—" My voice trails off. My heart is flickering with excitement. "I think I'm falling for him." I whisper, quiet and mumbled, a confession I wasn't ready to say, but it slipped out of my lips.

"Love?" Dalila says. "Celso? Have you got Stockholm syndrome?" She asks, laughing even louder than before.

"Ha. Ha. Funny." I throw the napkin at her and grin. "I'm serious."

Dalila's eyes soften as she stares across the table towards me. "I can see you are. And - as much as I'm still furious with Celso for what he did - I'm happy for you. I'm also a bit worried you understand. I mean I don't want to make things weird or make you worried - but it's Celso. I don't know. He's always been so - he's always been Celso." She shrugs.

I nod, I understand what she's trying to get at. I've always known Celso was trouble and her warning doesn't fall lightly. He's dangerous and unpredictable and I am still worried about him being obsessed because I'm something shiny and new - and when it wears off and I'm *me* - what will he do then?

"Be careful." She says a soft smile on her lips. "I want you to be happy, Neve, but be careful. I don't want you to get your heart broken."

I nod. "I am being careful. I know I have to be."

She's right. I'm falling way too deep, way too fast. It could all be an act, a game of some sort.

"Ugh." Dalila says, rolling her eyes and shaking her shoulders as though she is trying to shake off some weird vibe. "Let's not talk about my brother anymore." She grins. "Another cocktail? And I think you should get that bodycon dress we saw at Le Perla. It will be so hot with your new sneakers or a pair of heels. Win win."

"Alright. Another cocktail and this sushi is incredible." I pop another salmon rose into my mouth and wince when I taste it, I must have added a little too much wasabi.

Dali giggles.

Girls' day out is perfect. Talking to her gives me so much perspective regarding where my head is at - what direction my thoughts are going on. It's weird to admit that I am falling for Celso, and a little bit terrifying too. What if this is a game to him?

What if I'm the newest shiniest toy on his shelf and soon this is all going to wear off and I'll be - what will I be? What will happen to me when Celso gets bored?

"I don't think I can carry any more bags." Dalila laughs, adjusting her fingers around the shopping bags she has in her hands. "Shall we go back to the car? My feet are sore anyway. With the amount of walking, we did I feel like we could have climbed Everest."

I laugh at how dramatic she can be sometimes.

"Sure, my legs are tired too. I can head home and curl up on the sofa to watch a series."

"Yes, that's what I want to do too." She nods as we head towards the exit and out to the car.

The funny thing is that while Dalila chats about Nevio and what they've been up to, driving through the city with our windows open and the breeze whipping our hair into the air, my sunglasses down and the sunshine pressed against my skin - all I can think about is that I'm excited to get home and see Celso.

Home.

Because that's how I feel about his penthouse now. It feels like my home. It is my home.

And Celso - he's, my person. And I'm excited to be back with him.

I want to show him the cute things I bought, maybe even do a little fashion show for him. I want to tell him about how great the cocktails were and how we should definitely go to that place for sushi one day. I want to tell him I might be falling in love with him - but that - that would be stupid of me, wouldn't it?

A crazy little smile flickers across my lips as I enjoy the fresh air rushing into the car window. Dalila turns the music up and starts singing to an old Cranberries song. I join in, out of tune and too loud, my smile stretching all the way across my lips now.

I message Celso to tell him I'm on my way home and he replies with a little heart saying *I can't wait*.

When we pull up outside the building Celso is waiting downstairs for us. Dalila climbs out of the car, parked near the entrance, to help me unload my shopping bags. I bought half the amount she bought, but it still seems like way too much.

Celso walks over to help by taking the shopping bags and holding them in one hand. The other arm, he wraps around me so that he can pull me up close to him and kiss me.

"I missed you." He grins against my lips.

"I missed you too." I whisper.

"Gross." Dalila shouts, slamming the back door closed.

I let go of Celso and walk back over to her to hug her goodbye. "Thank you for an amazing day." I say.

"Yeah, yeah, get yourself back into the house so no one else has is being tortured with your gross lovey-dovey stuff." She laughs, pushing me away. She climbs into her car and waves as she leaves.

Celso pulls me towards the elevator, and we head up to our penthouse. I snuggle against him in the elevator, and he leans close to my ear and whispers "I can press the emergency stop button. We'd have at least twenty minutes before they got it going again." My cheeks flush pink and I glance at the security cameras.

"Actually, I thought I would do a little fashion show for you to show you what I bought today."

"Oh, really?" he asks surprised, his blue eyes narrowing as they stare down at me with mischief and curiosity. "Now, that sounds like what I want to be doing this evening." He pulls me close to kiss me again and my body sparks with desire.

I am genuinely happy to be with him again. I missed him today. It's so strange to miss him.

It's exciting and terrifying to feel this way about him.

It's Celso. Dalila's words whisper a warning in my mind.

CHAPTER TWENTY-TWO
Celso

I lean over the bed and gently kiss her cheek, waking her up how I've always dreamed of doing.

"My angel?" I whisper, brushing her hair from her face.

She blinks a few times. "Mm." Her sleepy little moan makes me want to climb back into bed with her.

"Why are you up so early, the sun isn't even awake?" She asks, her morning voice is husky and cute.

"Because we're going on an adventure today." I grin. "Your coffee is here." I wrap my arm around her back and lift her into a sitting position, as she snuggles her back against the pillows around the headboard and I hand her the coffee. Her hair is wild and messy around her shoulders. Fuck. She's sexy no matter what she does.

"An adventure?" She looks up at me with half-awake eyes and a curious smile.

"You're going to love it." I am trying not to give it away, but I'm so fucking excited about this.

My excitement infects her, and she wiggles a little, waking up.

"You've got plenty of time. Enjoy your coffee. Have a shower, do whatever you want to do - we need to leave here in just over an hour."

"Alright?" She says, smirking, drinking her coffee a little faster and starting to pull the blankets off.

"I said you have time." I laugh.

"I don't need time when there is an adventure waiting." She giggles, sliding out of bed and standing on her tiptoes to kiss me.

My heart tightens as I hold her against my body.

I almost say it. Right then and there. I almost tell her I love her. But this time the words get stuck in my throat. I know I've said it before. I've said it several times to her, but that was before I had her. Before she was my wife. The emotion I have inside me now is so much more intense. It's deeper, more intimate, and it fills my entire body.

I love her.

"Are you going to give me a clue?" she asks, her brows raised.

"No." I smirk.

"Nothing?" she huffs, still grinning.

"Zero."

She bites her lip and nods. "Ok, fine." She teases and hurries off to get ready.

Neve comes downstairs only twenty minutes later. Fresh for the day and wearing her blue jeans, a white cropped top, and her blue Nike hi-tops.

We climb into the car, and she hasn't stopped smiling even for a second.

"We're about half an hour early." I say, pulling over to stop at the bakery outside of town. A quaint little place run by an older couple, mostly used by people traveling longer journeys. "So, let's grab a takeaway coffee and a croissant. Do you want a chocolate one or a bacon one?" I ask.

"Um." She scrunches her nose.

"Both?"

She nods.

"I'll be right back."

The drive takes us out of the city and into the wide-open spaces and rolling hills of nature and mountains. It's beautiful and because we left even earlier than expected we are lucky enough to be driving right into the sunrise. Warm orange streaks paint the sky with hints of the adventure we are going on. Neve is going to be over the moon. I know it.

Sitting next to me in the car holding her croissant and nibbling at the edge in between sips of hot cappuccino in a takeaway mug - she is smiling and watching the sky ahead of us.

She leans over and presses on the stereo. Music fills the car, and she sings to it.

This is what I wanted for my life.

My life with her.

This is heaven to me.

It takes us an hour and a half to get to where we're going.

When I pull off the long open highway and down a dirt road Neve sits bolt straight in her seat. "Are we here?" She asks, her voice tight with excitement.

"We're here." I chuckle.

A mile down the road I pull off into a parking area, a wide gravel space with a concrete building ahead of us that looks like a bunker.

"What in the world?" Neve mutters, climbing out of the car, too impatient to wait for me to open the door for her.

I hurry out too because I want to see her face when she sees the surprise.

Grabbing her hand, I stop her from running ahead and she does a little skip next to me.

"It's just ahead - in the valley." I grin.

And when she sees it her face lights up like Guy Fox Day. Her eyes glittering with happiness.

The valley is a landing site for three different helicopters. I point to a black one with the word Hawk written on the side. "That is ours for today." I smile.

"We're going on a helicopter tour." She shouts.

"Yes, but also, today is your very first lesson in flying. You'll do simulation training, they are going to give you a book to study, you won't be allowed to fly the chopper yet, but we are going for a flight today."

She turns towards me, her mouth hanging open, her brows knotted.

"You - you signed me up for a lesson?"

"Yes, a package of lessons. In a few months you will be qualified to fly on your own. This base isn't the only one they have. They have one in the city too, so we won't have to drive out all the way here every time. But I wanted the first lesson to be out here because we have another surprise for this evening."

"I'll be a qualified pilot? I will be flying on my own?" She says in disbelief. For a moment I can't tell if she's scared or excited. I realize it's both.

"Do you want to do this?" I ask, nervous that I've made a mistake.

"*Are you fucking kidding me?*" She screams, jumping into my arms and covering my face in kisses. "This is freaking amazing. This is - this is - I can't—" she trips over her words, and I laugh at her outburst.

"Celso." She says my name, and it's a whisper of air. "This is amazing."

"Come on. Let's go meet your instructor."

Neve's first lesson is a few hours long. I relax by the pool near the training base and enjoy lunch at the restaurant and when she comes walking in with a smile that stretches across her entire face, her eyes glittering like diamonds and her chin held high and happy - my heart is filled with love at the sight of her.

She runs over to me when she spots me at the far table.

"Celso, it was amazing. The simulation is like being in a real helicopter. I was wearing VR goggles. I only crashed a few times. I mean that's not bad. Take off isn't as easy as you'd think it would be. And then the one time I got it going, and I was flying over the mountain tops, and it was so beautiful."

She sits down, letting out a heavy breath of air.

I can't stop grinning at her.

"I'm going to have some lunch, after that they are taking us flying - proper, real flying."

"That smile on your face - that's the smile I want to give you for the rest of your life." I say, pulling her chair closer to mine.

She leans her head onto my shoulder, and I wrap my arm around her, kissing the top of her head.

After steak rolls and caramel cake, we are on our way towards the Hawk chopper for the next step in our adventure.

Neve doesn't know it yet, but after a flight over the mountains we are getting dropped on top of the highest peak where they have a very exclusive, private house you can rent.

I've booked it for us for tonight. I've had them prepare dinner for us and stock the bar with champagne. A suitcase of our luggage was already taken from the trunk of my car where I packed it this morning while Neve was still sleeping - it's packed in the helicopter and will be dropped off with us.

The house we are staying in is made of glass, every wall is a view of the mountain ranges and wide-open skies. There is a hot tub, a natural waterfall running straight through the side of the house, a fireplace indoors, a bed that is built onto the side of the mountain so that you sleep on a cliff face, warm and safe in the glass walls - it's beyond incredible.

I can't wait to see her face when she sees that.

The helicopter ride is magnificent. We circle over the mountains and race through valleys while Neve squeals with excitement at the pilots' skills. At the end of our flight, she leans close to the window and points out the beautiful house on the mountain top and wonders who gets to live in such a magical place.

"Tonight - we do." I grin as the helicopter begins to descend. Headed for the landing pad carved into the mountain.

"Are you *serious?*" she asks in shock.

I nod.

She presses her face against the window again and stares in awe at our romantic getaway venue.

The pilot waves once we are out and standing on the platform. Wind whips her hair in a swirling, wild splash as he takes off again.

I hold her close.

Once we're completely and utterly alone, far away from everyone and everything, I lead her into the glass house.

She grabs my hand and explores every room and every corner, admiring the views from each point. Once we've seen the entire house we decide to soak in the hot tub and have champagne while we observe our mountain as though we are kings and queens.

The water is hot and a gentle drift of steams swirls over the surface as Neve floats towards me, her cheeks bright red from the heat and the champagne and all the excitement of today.

I reach out and pull her onto my lap. She floats over me, wrapping her thighs on either side of mine and she brushes her warm fingers over my cheeks, down my neck and wrapping them around the back of my shoulders.

"Today was - it was the best day of my life I think." She grins, leaning close, her lips brushing over mine.

"Marrying you was the best day of my life, Neve. It was the day my dream came true. The day I made you mine." My cock hardens beneath her, and she presses herself a little firmer onto my lap.

"Marrying you was - unexpected - for my heart."

"What do you mean by that?" I ask, a surge of excitement running through me.

"It means, I—" She bites her lip. I can see the nervous glimmer in her eyes.

"Neve?" I ask, pushing my finger underneath her chin and forcing her to look at me.

"It means that I didn't expect my heart to fall so madly in love with you." She whispers, the confession on her lips is like a volcano erupting inside my heart.

I can't speak, my throat tight with emotion and my heart beating so fast it might explode.

She leans her lips against mine and whispers. "I love you, Celso." And those words - her - everything - my body erupts with happiness.

I grab the back of her head and press her lips hard against mine. Love and desire mix as passion shoots through both of us. She moves, rocking against my hard cock, our naked bodies pressed together and the hot water splashing over the edges of the hot tub, flooding onto the wooden deck.

CHAPTER TWENTY-THREE
Neve

My heart is beating a million miles an hour when I find the courage to whisper those words to him.

I've been wanting to say it for so long now -

"I love you, Celso." I whisper against his lips as my heart beats even faster.

He grabs the back of my head and pushes his mouth over mine, locking me in place.

My body lights with fire inside my veins as I rock my hips, rubbing my pussy over his cock.

The passion of our skin is fueled with the passion of our hearts.

"You have no idea how long I've waited to hear that." He murmurs, his voice deep and husky, his words are a tease to my ears. "You do not know how long I've waited for you, Neve." He says and kisses me again, fierce, and wild, we move together in the hot tub out on the deck on the edge of the mountain.

Being here with him is some kind of dreamland. A fairy tale. The views, the bubbling water around us, the chilly evening air touching our skin.

His fingers thread into my hair and he pulls my head backwards, exposing my throat to his lips, he traces kisses over my skin.

"I've never seen anything more perfect than you." He growls, running his hand down my back, between my legs and brushing his fingers over my pussy.

I shudder in delight, and he lets his teeth grate along my neck as he pushes his fingers inside me, making me gasp.

"This pussy belongs to me." He snarls, pushing his fingers deeper. I can feel his cock pressing against me as well and I'm desperate for him to thrust it inside me.

I rock back and forth, rubbing myself against his hand.

He chuckles. "Mm. You love this don't you, my angel."

I nod and look at him with hungry eyes.

The muscles of his thick broad shoulders move and shift, shaped perfectly as he lifts his arm out of the water and traces his finger over my lips.

"Do you want me to fuck you?" He asks.

I nod, biting my lip.

A half smile curls the corner of his mouth. The dark shadow of stubble giving him a rugged, dangerous edge.

He lifts me up slightly, holding his cock, and lowers me down slowly onto it.

The moment he pushes into me I moan.

It's pure bliss as he pushes deeper, filling me up, forcing me open. My legs are stretched wide over him.

My muscles twitch around his massive cock and I lean forward, burying my face into his neck.

He wraps his hand around the back of my head, locking me against him and he begins to fuck me harder.

Water splashes around and I grip the edge of the hot tub.

Celso gets frustrated with not being able to thrust into me as hard as he wants to in the water, so he lifts me out and turns me around, pushing me face down over the edge of the tub.

He shoves his cock into me from behind and I squeal in delight as he grips my hips and fucks me as hard as he wants to.

His cock slams into me over and over again, steam drifting off my skin where the water meets the cooler night air.

I look up and all I see is a bright evening sky, filled with stars, over the silhouettes of mountains.

Everything is adding to the thrilling sensation of this experience.

It's almost overwhelming.

I can't seem to catch my breath I'm moaning so

much, gasping with each thrust, and enjoying the touch of his hands on my skin.

"Tell me again, angel. Tell me you love me." He growls.

"I love you." I gasp between breaths as he slams into me.

"And you belong to me." He says.

"I belong to you, Celso." I confess.

He grabs a handful of my hair his cock grows harder inside me.

I shudder with delight and my legs begin to shake as he fucks me faster and faster, pulling my hair and forcing me to arch my back towards him.

"Come on my cock, angel. I can feel you tightening."

He takes in a heavy breath. "Fuck that was so good." He growls as my orgasm rocks through me, making my pussy throb over his cock. Wave after wave of intense pleasure make me cry out and he pushes deep inside me, exploding while his moans vibrate against my back.

The night we make love again in the bedroom with glass walls, up against the edge of a mountain cliff, my heart beating fast from fear, adrenaline, and lust.

I sleep in his arms as soft mist dances over the views.

In the morning, we watch the sunrise and everything in my life has never been more perfect than it is right now.

I've never been happier or more free in my life. And I've never felt love like this before.

The way I feel about Celso makes me think that I've never understood love - not until I met a man who loves me for who I am.

I can't imagine my life without him.

Just before sunset the helicopter arrives to take us back to our car, and we take a road trip home. Both of us keep glancing at each other and smiling.

Everything has changed now. I don't have to hold back or fight how I feel about him. I've embraced it - along with the fears of what might happen -

I've let myself love him. I've let go and my heart has fallen deep down the rabbit hole.

The next two days at home are magical. Celso goes out of his way to do things for me, and I can't help but smother him in affection.

On Wednesday morning he has to go into work, and I'm left alone in the penthouse to keep myself busy.

While he is out the phone in his office rings, and I rush to answer it for him so that I can take a message.

I bolt up the stairs and pick it up in a hurry, but I'm too late and the line goes dead as I say hello.

"Oh well, they can call back if it's important." I mutter, setting the phone back in the cradle.

I bump his laptop and the screen flickers to life.

On the desktop I see a folder - the name of the folder is Neve.

I narrow my eyes and slowly sit down in his office chair. It must be our marriage certificate or something. Just a folder to keep things safe in.

It's not snooping if it's my name I'm clicking on.

I double click and it opens. There are so many files listed that at first, I'm confused. Why would he have so much information on me? One marriage certificate would make sense - but this - what is this?

I scroll down the list and click randomly.

A note pad opens with information about my college application. I wanted to go to a highly prestigious college as far from my father as possible. I wanted freedom. I remember the day the application was declined. It broke my heart.

I read through the notes and my stomach knots.

Celso tampered with my chances of getting in. It looks like he paid someone off to decline my application. Is this real? Why would he do that?

I click on another folder, my head beginning to spin with nausea.

This is a folder on the guy I liked two years ago. His name was Dylan. He was a nice guy.

I remember the day he broke up with me. He said I wasn't good enough for him and he told me I was boring and not that pretty. The cruel words were in such contrast to who I thought he was - to the guy I had gotten to know - it didn't make sense. But now it does. Celso paid him and threatened him - making sure he left.

File after file I click and sink deeper into depression and shock.

Three boyfriends - paid off.

The job I applied for in New York - tampered with.

College applications - ruined.

Every move I made to leave the city and every person I dated - or tried to date - Celso interfered with it.

There is a folder filled with incriminating images of my father. I knew it was him. I knew it and no one would listen to me.

My heart is shattered, falling to pieces. I can't breathe.

I get down to the bottom of the list and find a folder with Damion's name on it.

Intense anxiety washes over me as I hover the cursor above it.

Do I want to know?

Can I bear the truth of what I am about to see?

He has a voice recording of their conversation. A conversation that took place somewhere windy. Damion and Celso are arguing. Celso is trying to force Damion to take the money and leave. Disappear. Go live somewhere far away. Or take the money and break off the wedding.

Damion is laughing it off.

He says, "I don't have a choice. I have to marry her. My family is broke, and she is the only option I have. Do you think I want to do this? I don't want to get married. But I have to."

Celso snaps back, "She deserves someone who loves her. Someone who will give her the world. If you don't intend to do that, let her be with someone who deserves her."

"You? You think you deserve her. Fuck off man. You can have her when I'm done with her. Once my family gets the money, we need out of her family I'll divorce her, and she'll be all yours."

That's when Celso loses his mind and Damion screams.

I listen, frozen in my seat. Damion begging him to stop.

Celso growling and snarling with effort. Then Damion goes silent.

He tried to pay him off, and the deal went wrong, and he ended up murdering him.

Celso murdered Damion.

I can't breathe.

Every single thing that has gone wrong in my life has been because Celso interfered. I didn't even open half of the folders, but I can't bring myself to look at another thing.

I've seen what I need to see, and it's enough to make me realize - Celso is the monster I always thought he was.

He is a murderous asshole who only cared about what he wanted. He interfered with my life, repeatedly until he ended up destroying my father and killing the man I was supposed to marry.

Tears are streaming down my cheeks when I stand up. My legs are weak and shaking. I grip the side of the desk and try to steady myself but I'm struggling.

Celso walks into the office.

"Neve? What are you doing in here?" His voice is tight, strained.

"You killed him. You did - you did so many terrible things." I mumble, still fighting for air.

"Neve, sit down, my angel, you're pale." He hurries around the desk and tries to wrap his arm around me, but I scream and push him away. The anger giving me some clarity and a chance to take a deep breath. "Don't touch me. You are a monster. You've - you've been controlling my life." I shout.

"Neve, please, if you let me explain—"

"Explain what? How? Nothing you say will make this ok."

I can't stop crying. I'm scared, but I'm angrier than anything else.

My heart rate is through the roof and my fists are clenched at my side.

CHAPTER TWENTY-FOUR
Celso

Right now, staring at Neve as she tries to hold herself together, I can see the pain I've caused. I can see the damage I've done, and my mind is in overdrive trying to figure out how to fix it.

"Neve, I did it because I couldn't be without you. I couldn't let you leave the city. I couldn't let you go to college somewhere far away from me. Don't you get it? I need you here. I can't be without you. I did this all so that we can be together - and we're happy now—"

She shakes her head as I try to step towards her again.

"Don't you dare touch me." She snarls. "You've done all of this for *yourself*. You didn't do this for me. You did this so that you could get what you wanted. How do you know I wouldn't have been happier with any of those other guys? How do you know it wasn't my dream to go to that college? You made the choices for me. You have been manipulating my life for years." She's so angry her face is bright red from shouting.

I can see her hands shaking and the tears are streaming down her cheeks and soaking her white top.

"My angel." I mutter, breaking apart inside. "Please, try to understand why—"

"There is no way that justifies murder - and what you did to my father." She stammers in disbelief.

"Your father - all I did was show the world who he was. And Damion - he said the most terrible things about you. He was using you and your family. He didn't care about you at all. No one has a right to speak about you like that. And you would have ended up trapped in a marriage to that man."

"That may be so." She says. "But you - you." She breaks down, her voice snapping and her words no longer audible. Neve pushes past me as she hurries to our bedroom.

I follow close behind her. Wanting to help her. Wanting to comfort her, but the hate in her eyes dares me to even come close to her without consequences.

Neve grabs a suitcase out of the closet and starts throwing clothing into it.

"Don't leave. I'm begging you don't leave me." I drop to my knees and wrap my hands over my eyes. "Please, Neve. You don't understand. If you leave, I will be destroyed. I will have no reason left to live."

She turns to glare at me.

"I can't be here right now, Celso. I can't bear the sight of you."

She grabs the handle of the suitcase and storms from the bedroom. I can't move. I can't stand up and I can't turn to watch her walk away.

The front door closes with a bang and there is silence.

Heavy, empty, stony silence.

The only thing I've ever wanted - I just lost.

The most precious thing in the entire world has walked out of my life and I don't think she will ever speak to me again.

I should have deleted that folder. I should have made sure she could never find out.

But somewhere deep inside me I left it there so that she could stumble upon it.

Somewhere deep inside me I wanted her to know who I really was - and I wanted her to love me, anyway.

I wanted her to love me despite the darkness I can sense, drifting through my veins. The bitter heart I have towards anything that isn't her.

She is the reason I don't have to be that person. She is the only thing that holds the darkness at bay and the reason I have to be better.

Without her - without the chance of ever having her again - I am a monster.

I am nothing but a demon.

The dark ache that begins to consume me is thick like oil. It floods through my body, heavy and pitch black until I can't see or think straight. I can't do anything but let rage take over.

I was never good enough for her.

That's the truth.

She is the angel, and I am the devil.

What right did I ever have to think I deserved something so pure.

So beautiful.

So perfect.

I drag myself to my feet and blindly make my way out of the penthouse, down to the parking garage. I shouldn't leave. I should stay home. I am dangerous right now and there is no telling what I might do.

But I don't care.

Without Neve - nothing matters.

Maybe my father did kill my mother - and I have his blood in my veins - meaning I am doomed to hurt the woman I love more than anything in the universe.

Maybe it's true.

After all, I am my father's son.

I stand in the center of the dance floor of the club I saw Neve in. I know she won't be here, but it's somewhere she has been - and therefore I can feel her somehow.

Music pulses through my body along with the many shots of tequila I've had. My vision is blurred. I had hoped that the alcohol would numb me, but it's only turned me darker.

My soul is in the pits of hell. My heart doesn't exist without her.

Someone shoves me from behind and I turn, swinging my fist before I even see who it is. The bouncer takes the hit and snarls like a wild animal.

"What the fuck are you doing back here?" He growls, grabbing me as I throw pinches left, right, and center.

I don't even know what I'm doing.

I'm rabid. Psychotic. Screaming and hitting at nothing and everything.

It takes three of them to toss me out into the curbside. I roll onto my side, breathing heavily.

I can smell the alcohol on my breath.

Pushing myself to my feet I laugh with manic anger. The bottle store across from the club is still open so I stagger inside and buy a bottle of vodka. I will numb this pain. I don't care how much I have to drink to make that happen. I can't feel like this. I can't bear it. I have to stop this ache in my chest, in my stomach, in my arms and legs.

I tear the bottle top off as soon as I step back out onto the streets.

Downing half the bottle in one breath.

Someone walks past and asks me if I'm trying to kill myself.

"Yes." I hiss. "Yes, I deserve to die. And without her there is no reason to live, anyway." I snarl at him, and he steps away from me with his hands in the air. "For Fuck sakes buddy. Fine." He hurries away and I stagger towards my car with the open bottle in my hand.

Yanking the door open I catch a whiff of her.

Her scent is trapped inside my car. I fall to my knees on the pavement, clutching at my chest.

The pain is too much.

I can't get into the car.

I can't be anywhere she has been.

How can I lie in our bed tonight when I will be able to smell her on the pillows?

I stand up and sway as I stare into the car.

Fuck this.

Fuck the universe and fuck the indescribable pain I feel in my body.

I throw the bottle of vodka into the car, and it smashes against the inside of the passenger door. I dig around in my pocket, looking for my zippo.

One strike. A flame dances in my hand.

Perhaps I understand why Rufino did what he did.

I toss the lighter into the car and a heat wave explosion throws me off my feet.

Sitting on the sidewalk I watch the flames consume the inside of my car.

Thick smoke starts to pour out of the open driver's door.

I can't stop laughing.

It's so beautiful.

It's so destructive.

I want to throw myself into those flames so that they can consume my pain, but I can't move.

Hands grab at me, dragging me away from the wall of heat pouring from the car.

"What the fuck, are you ok? What happened?"

I push the people away from me and turn away from the chaos.

Without a word, I run.

I keep running until I can't breathe and still, I run some more.

Perhaps I can run myself to death.

I run until I reach the city center, the park. It's dark, lit by tall, ornate lamps that spill pools of light in bright circles breaking up the pitch darkness of the night.

I walk along the tree line, staring into the manmade forest, wondering what horrors lurk between the thick trunks.

I must have blacked out at some point because I wake up to a homeless man kicking me.

"Hey, asshole, you're in my spot. This is my spot. I have been coming here for years. You can't come here and take someone else's spot." He reeks of booze and sweat. Or maybe it's me.

I groan as I sit up, finding myself on a bench in the very early hours of dawn.

Light is glowing over the horizon, the sun threatening to welcome in a new day.

I stand up, finding myself still drunk.

"Hey, hey, you can't leave. Maybe you can give me some food first. I won't buy wine. I swear it. I just want food."

Shoving my hand into my pocket I fish out my wallet.

I take the entire wad of cash out, a couple of thousand, and hand it to the man.

"What? Is this a joke?" he asks, staring at his hands.

I'm surprised no one mugged me while I was passed out, anyway.

"No joke." I mutter, closing my eyes for a second to hold the headache at bay.

The homeless man is still talking when I walk away.

I need to get home and shower.

I need to find Neve. I need to fix this. I can't give up.

I won't stop until I know I've exhausted every option of getting her back.

She is my wife. She is my world, and I want her. I want her by my side. I want to love her.

I want to be loved by someone so pure and so beautiful.

I might not deserve it - but I will fight for it.

I get home and Rufino and Masaccio are waiting for me.

"Fuck, Celso. What happened? Your car blew up. Did someone attack you?" they ask.

"I did it." I mutter, pushing past them into my penthouse.

"What the fuck do you mean you did it."

I chuckle and glance at Rufino. "Ask the Red Dragon. He'll understand."

"Where's Neve?" Rufino asks.

"She left." I chuckle.

"Fuck." Rufino says, looking at Mas with deep lines of concern etched into his forehead.

"What happened? We can try to help you solve it. Things are going to be ok, Celso." Rufino says, stepping towards me with his hand out.

"She's gone, Rufino. She found out who I really am, and she ran away as fast as she could. She doesn't want me. It's over." I laugh and I can hear how crazy I sound, but I have no control over it. The laughter begins to consume me until I collapse onto the sofa, clutching my stomach.

"Call the doctor." Masaccio says, putting his hand on my shoulder. "Celso, breathe man."

But all I can do is laugh. Tears streaming down my face. I'm laughing so much it hurts, but I can't stop.

"We need to have him sedated before he does something stupid." Masaccio says.

"You mean like drinking a whole bottle store or blowing up his own car?" Rufino says gruffly, his phone pressed against his ear.

"Hey doc, we need you at Celso's place." I listen as he paces up and down and tells the doctor about how I am having a psychotic breakdown.

He's not wrong.

Laughter continues to shake through me.

CHAPTER TWENTY-FIVE
Neve

"You need to go back." My brother snaps, throwing his hands in the air.

"Go back and tell him you forgive him, Neve. You can't do this to us."

He is marching up and down the living room at my father's house.

"How can you say that?" I say angrily and heated. "I told you he messed with my college applications - and he paid my boyfriends to leave—" I stammer in disbelief. Luke doesn't seem to be in the least bit bothered about what I'm explaining to him.

I haven't told Luke about what happened with Damion - or my father.

He doesn't need to know everything.

But I told him enough to make any normal person cringe and tell me to stay far, far away from Celso.

"It doesn't matter, Neve, you have to go back. He'll pull the funding. He will stop helping the campaign. Our family will lose everything. All the work and time I've put into it will be for nothing."

"Luke, you want me to go back there even though he has broken my trust in the most terrifying way possible?" Tears sting my eyes and drift down my cheeks. "I'm telling you that my *husband*, the man I fell in love with, betrayed me and broke my heart - and all you can think about is your campaign?" I whisper, pained that my brother hasn't once asked me if I'm ok.

He hasn't put his arm around me to hug me or comfort me.

In fact, the moment I arrived at his door with my suitcase he started trying to convince me to go back.

Luke runs his hand through his hair and sighs, agitated. Annoyed by my pain.

"Can't you stay with him until the campaign is getting stronger and I can find another person to fund it?" he asks, raising his brows in a hopeful glance.

I shake my head. I can't believe he is doing this to me. I don't know why I thought he would understand and want to be there for me.

"Fuck you, Luke." I snap, standing up and walking away from him. "Fuck you for being like dad. You don't care about anyone or anything except for your stupid fucking campaign."

"Neve, we have to think about the family—" he shouts after me, but I'm done listening.

I storm all the way up the stairs to my bedroom and slam the door behind me.

I hate it here. Being here brings back all the memories of how I was oppressed and controlled by my family's expectations of me.

The good girl.

Be perfect.

Smile for the media.

Wear this.

Say this.

Do this.

I flop face first down onto my bed and let the heavy, miserable sobs fall out of me and onto my pillow. staining salty patches onto the soft fabric.

My brother doesn't give a shit about what I'm going through.

My father wouldn't have either.

Even Damion wasn't the man I thought he was. He was his own kind of evil.

All these men who I thought were good men - not a single one of them cared about me.

And the man who cares about me is a complete monster. He might not have directly hurt me, but he's done things that have changed the course of my life.

I cry until I pass out and when I wake up, I have a thunderous headache.

It's dark outside and I'm cold, lying on the bed without the blankets over me.

Reaching over I pick up my phone to see what the time is.

Three AM.

I slept for seven hours. I didn't expect that.

Sighing I roll over and sit up, rubbing my eyes with my fingertips. I need a painkiller and some water. I'm also hungry, even though I don't know if I can eat with my stomach knotted this way. I'll hurl if I try.

My phone chimes and I glance at it. The screen is bright in the darkness of my bedroom.

Celso.

I sigh and pick it up to read the message.

> Celso: I know you are angry, and you have every right to be. I'll be lucky if you even take the time to read this. But please, don't give up on me, angel. I did everything for you. I did everything because I thought, right or wrong, that we were meant to be together, and I had to make it happen. It's all I have ever wanted, and it's still all I want. Give me a chance. I will prove to you that nothing else matters. I will prove to you that when I have you, I don't have to be that monster because I don't have to fight for what I want - if I have you, I have everything.

> Please. Give me a chance, my angel. I love you. I will never stop loving you until I take my last breath.

I swallow hard, trying to push away the lump in my throat. I can't cry anymore. My head hurts too much, and crying will make my headache worse.

The worst part is that I love him too.

I hate what he's done to me, and I don't think I

will ever get over it. I can't trust him. But I love him.

I love him more than anything.

I want to be with him more than anything.

My phone drops from my fingers onto the blankets next to me. I can't reply. I wouldn't even know what to say.

It's dark and quiet while I walk around my father's house. Thinking, trying to work out what I want, trying to figure out how to heal my heart.

I walk until around five in the morning and then curl up on the sofa downstairs, falling asleep again.

A loud knock on the door wakes me up with a fright.

I sit up, bolt upright, my heart beating wildly.

The person knocks again, and I rush over to see who it is while I run my fingers through my hair to tame it.

Opening the door, I glance up and down, taking in the sight of a delivery man holding a giant bunch of flowers and a big box.

"Are you - uh - Mrs. Vece?" he asks, looking at his phone, trying to balance everything.

Mrs. Vece. I belong to him.

I take a deep breath. "Yes, that's me."

"Here you go." He says, handing me the flowers. "Where can I put this?" he gestures to the box. "It's heavy."

I lead him into the foyer, and he sets it down on the entrance table then nods and leaves.

I am not opening that box. It's from Celso.

I hear Luke coming down the stairs, he's on the phone having a heated discussion with one of his campaign managers. "If he pulls funding, we're fucked. Listen - we need to fish around—" I sigh, turning my attention back to the box.

Fine. I'll open it. But first I'll put these flowers in a vase. There is no point in their beauty going to waste because I'm angry with the man who sent them.

I brush my fingers over the delicate petals of blue, pink, and yellow.

The scent of sweet pollen fills the air.

My heart aches.

I fight tears.

When the flowers are soaking in a vase on the coffee table in the living room, I go back to pick up the box and carry it up to my bedroom. It's not that heavy.

Luke is on another call. He's stressing and pacing around the house. I can't stand it. He didn't even glance at me or say good morning. His only focus is the campaign, and his only worry is that Celso will pull funding.

In my room my phone light is blinking to tell me I have unread messages.

I set the box on my bed and read through Celso's messages.

One after another. He tells me I'm beautiful. He tells me I'm perfect. He tells me he wants nothing more than for me to be happy - no matter what that means.

My heart breaks over and over again as I read his words because he is the person who made me happier than I have ever been. He is the person who I want to be with - I don't know how.

I set my phone aside, not replying.

In the box I find jewelry, chocolates, clothing, shoes.

I sigh, closing the lid again.

I wish I knew what to do.

If it were up to me - I would force my heart to forgive him. I would give him another chance. But what risk would that involve? It seems like the worst choice to make.

But how can I go through my life without at least taking that risk?

Celso was the first person ever who let me be myself.

He is the first person ever who put me first - over everything else. Above his work, above his needs and wants - he put me first.

My heart clenches and I cry again.

I have to find a way through this.

Two days drift by in a fog. I can't think straight. My heart is getting heavier the longer I try to stay away from Celso. I keep crying and I am completely and utterly lost.

And he has continued to send gifts and messages.

This morning a customized four by four Jeep arrived for me. It has a full body kit, full off-road gear and even one of those roof top tents built into the roof racks.

The note attached to the steering wheel said," *for the adventures we might have in the future." I want to drive far and get lost with you. I want to sleep under the stars and make wishes when they shoot across the sky. I want to watch the moon and swim in wild rivers. I love you, my angel, and I will never give up.*

The letter got to me more than anything else.

Those are the exact things I want to do.

All my life I've been trying to escape these walls, these expectations, these rules for my life.

All my life I've been looking for someone like Celso to share my hopes and dreams with. Now I found him, through some crazy, awkward, wild coincidence the universe gave me everything I ever wanted - and then took it away.

Except - it didn't take it away.

Celso is still very much here, very much fighting for me. He hasn't given up and doesn't seem like he intends to.

How many kinds of stupid would I be if I gave up on a man who is willing to do so much to win me back?

And everything he did - everything that drove me away from him when I found out - all of those things saved me in a way. Each thing he did to control my life ended up benefiting me. Marrying Damion would have been hell. Going to a college I only wanted to attend to escape my father - it was a stupid idea.

Each of those idiots I dated were all approved by my father.

My life has not been my own, not until I met Celso.

I should at least talk to him.

I don't have to make any decisions - I can go see him and see how it makes me feel when I'm there.

My heart constricts in my chest.

I know how it will make me feel.

Because I am still madly in love with him.

I'm terrified of letting myself admit that.

CHAPTER TWENTY-SIX
Celso

After I had a mental breakdown Mas and Rufino had the doctor dose me up with sedatives and I slept like a rock for twelve hours straight.

When I woke up Rufino was sitting next to my bed.

He told me what he went through, all the fires and all the damage and how he almost killed the woman he loves. He told me not to be stupid and to figure out a different way to fix this.

After that I pulled myself together at least somewhat and I've been patiently doing everything I can to communicate with Neve and win her back into my life. Perhaps not as patiently as I would like, but I'm trying.

I haven't seen her in a week, and I don't know how much more of this I can handle.

I haven't been eating well, and I have barely been sleeping.

Rufino has been checking in with me daily, but I have nothing to tell him. The truth is I'm falling apart.

It's late afternoon and I'm sitting on my sofa, staring out of the window at nothing at all.

I hear my door unlocking and my entire body goes tense.

It must be Rufino. Fuck. I need to relax. They have the spare key to my penthouse for emergencies.

"Hey man, I'm in here." I call out when the door opens.

"Celso?" there is a pause. "I let myself in - um - I still have the key."

Her voice. It rings through the air like the sweetest, most beautiful melody I've ever heard.

I leap out of the sofa and run into the foyer.

Not giving it a moment's thought I grab her in my arms and hold her against me, burying my face in her soft, silky hair.

She is stiff in my embrace. But I can't find it in myself to let her go.

"Celso." Her voice is soft, uncertain.

I step back with difficulty. Neve is dressed in white sweatpants, her blue Nike sneakers, and a blue crop top. She looks gorgeous, as cute as ever, but her eyes are tired.

There are dark shadows beneath them, and it breaks my heart to see her like this.

I glance down at myself. I haven't left the house in days. I am a wreck.

Brushing my hands over my clothes, I clear my throat self-consciously.

"Neve - you're here." is all I can say, my throat tight and stiff around all the words I want to say to her.

"I came to talk." She says, taking a little step away and creating space between us.

"Sure, come in, can I get you something to drink? A coffee? A whiskey? A glass of fresh orange juice?" I'm rambling. I need to shut up.

"Can we talk?" She asks, biting her lip.

I nod, gesturing for her to go through to the living room. I follow behind her, my eyes taking in every movement, my mind wandering if I am hallucinating.

She sits on the couch, on the edge of the seat, looking uncomfortable and as though she might get up and run out at any second.

I pace up and down near the window.

"Neve, I'm so sorry." I blurt out. "I never wanted to hurt you. I only wanted - I wanted you and I did crazy, stupid things to get you. I can't even tell you that if I had to do it all again, I wouldn't be as stupid - I probably would." I sigh, brushing my hand through my hair.

I'm nervous. My shoulders are tense.

"Can you sit down, you're giving me anxiety." She murmurs, taking a deep breath.

"Sorry." I sigh, sitting in the seat opposite her even though I want to sit next to her and drag her onto my lap. I want to hold her and never let go. I could lock the doors and keep her prisoner -

Fuck.

I want to do that so badly.

But where will it get me?

She wouldn't be able to still love me.

Maybe she already doesn't love me anymore.

I stare across the space between us, watching her, waiting, giving her time to say what she came here to say - but she's quiet.

Neve fidgets, her hands in her lap, her fingers twisting through each other. She scrunches her nose. "I think I will have some tea." She says, looking for a distraction.

I jump up, eager to give her anything she wants.

She follows me through to the kitchen and leans against the counter while I make the tea.

I can see her struggling to piece her thoughts together, so I do my best to stay quiet.

"Celso, you need to stop sending me those gifts." She says.

"I can't. Even if you're not here, I still want to give you everything you've ever wanted."

"I don't want gifts I want—" She pauses. "I want someone I can trust. Someone I depend on."

I clench my jaw, the muscles rippling across my face.

"I will earn your trust back. The truth is you needed to find out those things - I didn't want to hide any part of myself from you, Neve. I always hoped that you would see me for exactly who I am and love me, anyway." I turn to face her, and her eyes are wide and gentle.

She's looking at me as though I've said something profound.

"That's what I always wanted too." She takes the tea from me. "I wanted someone to love me for who I am and not who they want me to be."

"Neve - I love you. I love you as you are. And if you want to change and dye your hair purple and get tattoos everywhere - I will still love you for who you are. You have the most beautiful soul, the most beautiful heart - I want *you*. I *need* you."

She smiles as she raises her eyes up towards me. "You kind of look like shit." She chuckles.

"Ouch." I smirk. "But you look like you are getting around about the same amount of sleep I'm getting?"

She pulls her mouth and scrunches her nose again. "Zero?"

"Yeah, about zero. It's starting to affect me. In fact, I'm a little worried I'm hallucinating you. Are you really here?" I grin as though I'm joking but I step forward to touch her face. To see if she's real.

She reaches up and brushes her fingers over my hand and sparks fly between us like static electricity.

"Please let me love you, my angel." I ask.

"I - I want to - I'm scared."

"Of what?" I ask.

She swallows and looks into my eyes. "Of you, Celso." She whispers.

Her words make my legs weak because of all the things in the world I know I would never harm her. But I did. I hurt her. I broke her heart.

Shit. I screwed things up by keeping it from her. I should have told her myself. Instead of letting her find it on her own.

"Neve, those things that I did - I would never do that if you belonged to me. But I will also never stop fighting for you. So as long as you are out there - and not by my side - I will do whatever it takes to get you back."

"Celso." She says, frustrated. "You can't go around controlling my life."

"I won't have to if you tell me, you love me and you will come back to me." I huff.

"You say you will never hurt me, but you went through so much to get me - and we got married - and what if all of that crazy passion burns out - you are capable of some stuff I don't understand - and there is no saying what you might do to me when you get bored with me." She finally lets me know what she is terrified of.

I close the space between us, leaning against her and pressing her into the kitchen counter. I grab her jaw in my hand and lift her head towards me.

"You are my everything. For eternity. I want you forever and no one - ever - will replace you or steal my attention. I might be a little crazy. But that I know for sure."

Her breathing has become heavier, faster. Her pupils are dilated.

I can sense it. The desire. The heat building between us.

Leaning down I press my lips over her mouth and kiss her.

She doesn't resist. My body sparks to life. Like I have not felt since the day she left me.

Neve lets out a quiet whimper and pushes her hand against my chest. Gently, almost reluctant.

I release her and step away, my heart sinking to the pit of my stomach.

"I should go." She whispers, brushing her fingers across her lips as though she wants to hold on to our kiss.

"Will you reply to my messages when I message you? I can't handle the silence anymore." I ask.

She nods. "Sure. If I'm near my phone, we can chat. Sometimes."

The knot in my stomach tightens.

"Neve please give me a chance. One more chance."

"I'll see you soon, maybe." She says politely, turning to leave.

"Oh, here." She says, holding out her hand to give the house keys back to me.

"Keep them. Just in case."

She bites her lip and nods and drops the keys into her purse.

"Bye Celso."

"Goodbye, my angel."

This time I watch her walking away, and it shatters me, but it also makes me more determined. My mind is made up. I will have her.

I'll give her some time, but if she doesn't choose me on her own, I will kidnap her. She needs some time with me to remind her of how good we are together.

We are perfect for each other.

When Neve is gone, I sit on the sofa again, staring, thinking, trying to understand.

Perhaps I am playing this the wrong way.

Perhaps what she needs is space from me. No messages, no gifts, no reminders of who I am to her - and what she is to me.

Just silence.

I can watch her from a distance.

What I saw tonight, and even her coming here - it tells me she still wants this. She could have dropped the keys on the kitchen counter - but she kept them. She could have messaged me to leave her alone - but she hasn't.

Neve is still in love with me. She is struggling with the moral dilemma of what I did to win that love from her.

But that isn't her karma to bear. That is mine.

So, I stalk her again. Like I used to in the past, right in the beginning when she hardly knew my name. I follow her when she goes to the shops. I follow her when she walks at the park.

When she gets coffee in town, I am sitting close, always watching.

I park outside her father's house - Luke's house - and I watch her moving around inside.

It's thrilling, sparking my desire for her to an entirely new level. It becomes darker, more determined.

I will have her.

One way or another.

No one else will ever touch her - she is mine. She will always be mine.

CHAPTER TWENTY-SEVEN
Neve

I can't stop thinking about him.

No matter what I do.

No matter where I go or how much I try to distract myself. I can't get Celso out of my mind or my heart.

I'm falling apart without him. And I'm terrified of being with him.

In the last few days, he hasn't messaged me and I'm worried.

What if he's given up? He said he never would though. What if he has?

The thought shatters me. It makes me realize that I never wanted him to give up because I always knew that at some point I would give in and go back to him.

I belong with him.

I need time to process everything.

I could be wrong though. After what I found out about him.

It could be my heart tricking my mind. Matters of logic falling away while blind love leads me. Dammit.

I need to talk to Dalila. She will know what to do. She always does.

Grabbing my phone off my bedside table I lie on my back, holding it above my head while I type the message to Dalila.

> Me: I need to talk. I need to get out. I need my friend.

> Dalila: Finally. I'm glad you're done saying no to my invites. I'll come fetch you at eight. Dinner first and then we're going dancing.

> Me: I'm not in the mood for a club. Dinner sounds perfect.

> Dalila: I don't care. Wear something hot. We are going dancing.

I grin and shake my head.

> Me: Fine. I'll be ready at eight.

Dalila arrives at Seven thirty. Nevio drops her off. We are going to catch an Uber there so that we don't have to worry about having a few drinks.

She waltzes into my room like it's her own. "You aren't even close to ready." She shakes her head, looking me up and down where I'm standing in a towel, fresh out of the shower.

"I almost canceled three times already." I sigh, throwing my hands in the air in frustration.

"Idiot." She mutters, walking over to the closet, tugging it open and searching through my dresses. "Oh, wow, this is new." She says holding up a deep blue sequin dress.

"Celso got it for me." I sigh. "It was one gift he had sent over here."

"Well, if there is one thing I can say about my brother it's that he has good taste." She tosses the dress onto the bed and searches through my shoes, selecting gold stilettos.

"Um. No." I shake my head at the shoes. She rolls her eyes.

"These?" She holds up a pair of red bottom black, strappy stilettos. I nod.

"Ok. Well, hurry." She waves her hand over the clothes and heads into my bathroom to find a hairbrush.

I slip into the dress and Dalila comes out and grabs my shoulders, turning my back to her and starting to tug my hair up into a messy, wild, loose bun high on my head.

I don't know what all the worry was about.

We walk out of my room at eight on the dot.

Sitting at the restaurant I relax. I really didn't want to come out. I changed my mind so many times and grappled between forcing myself to go and cancelling and climbing into bed. Never mind being late - if Dalila hadn't rocked up when she did, I would have messaged her and said no.

"Girl, you need to talk to me. You've been way too quiet for way too long and it's not good for you." Dalila says, pouring me a glass of white wine. She's already ordered salmon for us with vegetables and baby roast potatoes on the side.

"I'm so lost." I shrug. "Most of the time I don't even understand what's going on in my head so how can I explain it to someone else." I chew at the inside of my cheek, uncomfortable and not wanting to cry in public.

Dalila tilts her head to the side. "Ok, so you found out some crazy stuff he did in the past right? And you left."

I nod.

"And now - are you happy you left but angry with him? Are you scared he's going to do something to you - because if he hurts you, I swear I will—"

"No. No it's not like that." I mutter.

Dalila picks up her wine and sips it while she watches me thoughtfully.

"Neve, the thing is that with whatever happened - we can all have our own opinions, but you are the only one who knows what happened between you two - and you are the only one who knows what you want at the end of the day."

"What do you mean?" I ask, knotting my brows.

"I mean - you should follow your heart. Trust your heart. And no matter what I say or what your brother says - or even what my brother says - you should do what makes you happy."

"I thought you didn't want me anywhere near Celso."

She grins.

"So, you *do* want to be with him still?" she says, drawing attention to my obvious statement. A confession I hadn't realized I'd made.

My mouth drops open. "Um, I didn't say that exactly—"

"If you fell in love with that idiot - well that's your own stupidity." Dalila giggles. "Ok, no, but in all seriousness, Neve. I want you to be happy. With Celso or without Celso. I want you to be happy."

Her saying that is a massive weight being lifted off my shoulders.

I have her blessing either way. I can walk away and hurt her brother, or I can go back to him - and she will still accept me as her friend.

"Ok, let's not talk about this anymore. I want to have some fun tonight and relax."

"Yes. Clear your head. Eat good food. Dance and forget about boys for tonight." Dalila lifts her wine glass and holds it towards me.

The club is packed. It's so loud I can't hear Dalila when she asks me what I want to drink. She waves her hand in the air to say *never mind* and orders us some shots. After three shots I am relaxed and buzzing. The music is freaking incredible, the heavy bass is massaging my brain into silence and I'm smiling for the first time in what seems like forever.

I dance, and I keep dancing until my feet ache. Dalila leads us to the bar to get more drinks.

That's when I see him.

He's standing by the bar with his eyes on me.

My heart leaps into my throat and my stomach is swarming with butterflies, all taking off at once.

I can't look away and our eyes lock for the longest time. He smiles, the slightest curve of his lips, almost unperceivable.

Instead of rushing over to greet him, I take my shot, play it cool and head back to the dance floor.

But I can't stop looking in his direction and the more I watch him the more I want to talk to him. But he'll come and talk to me, surely. He'll come say hi or dance with me. He always does.

Dalila noticed him because she followed my gaze. All she did was roll her eyes.

She's dancing next to me and is oblivious to the heavy tension in the air between Celso and me.

After the most recent round of shooters glitters my brain, I can't hide my smile when I look towards him.

He licks his lips and every cell in my body flares.

Fuck he's hot. Like crazy hot. Like wildly, inappropriately, can't be real hot.

I flirt with him by dancing and teasing a little. I'm playing with fire but I'm having fun. And I need a little fun in my life right now.

For an hour Celso and I flirt silently across the club. He sips his drink, his eyes wandering over me, and I wait for him to come over and say something to me.

After a while I tire of waiting, annoyed that he isn't chasing me like he has. He hasn't been messaging me the last few days. He hasn't been sending gifts, and now he's at the club and basically ignoring me.

What is going on with him?

What is he even doing here? Is he here by accident and I happened to be here?

I chew the inside of my cheek, impatient, frustrated with him for keeping his distance.

I turn my back on him to hide my expression. My brows knotted while I try to decide if I'm going to march over there and give him a piece of my mind or not.

When I turn back - he's gone.

I wait for him to come back.

But he's gone.

He freaking left the club.

He didn't say hello, and he didn't say goodbye and when I realize that my heart shatters.

Also - anger floods me like a wild rainstorm.

Dalila leans close to me, shouting right into my ear. "One last drink - Nevio is on his way to pick us up."

"I'm going to catch a taxi, actually."

"Why? That's stupid. We can drop you at home."

"I'm not going home." I shout back, trying to be heard over the bass. I'm angry, fired up and ready to confront him for walking away without saying a word to me.

She grins and rolls her eyes. "Ok, I get it." She laughs. "Well, wait here with me until Nevio gets here and we can drop you at Celso's place."

I smirk, she knows me too well. I guess that is what friends are for. She didn't even judge me for trying to sneak off without telling her. "Thanks." I grin and she orders us one more drink while we wait for Nevio to arrive.

I stand on the sidewalk outside Celso's building. "Thank you, drive safe." I shout back into the car. I swing it closed. The door slams a little harder than I expect it to, and I jump in fright. I need to calm down. Sheesh. Dalila grins and shouts goodbye through the open window and Nevio waves.

My stomach knots tightly as I walk towards the entrance of Celso's building.

I'm still angry.

I can't believe he left.

Digging around in my purse I find my house keys,

which luckily have his house keys attached to them.

I'm tipsy. Perhaps more than tipsy. My head spins while the elevator takes me up to the top floor.

"Asshole." I mutter to no one. "How can you watch me for an hour and leave?" My anger rises, pushing away the anxiety and nerves. I'm definitely going to give him a piece of my mind when I get up there. He's going to hear exactly what I think about him and his stupid games. And who the hell does he think he is not messaging me or calling for the past few days?

It's not acceptable.

The elevator doors slide open, and I have to hold on to the wall for a moment to steady myself. Wow. I should not have had that last drink, but I'm also giggling because I'm still having more fun than I've had in ages. Well, since I left Celso. It's nice not to be drowning in my misery and to instead be a little tipsy and on my way to give someone a mouthful of drama.

I fumble with the key and fumble again and swear loudly.

The door opens and Celso is standing there in a pair of dark jeans - and nothing else.

I stare up at him and narrow my eyes. My body ignites as my eyes trace over his perfection. Fuck. What was I going to say?

"Angel. What are you doing here?" he says, his deep voice a smooth current washing away my anger.

"I - I came to - you should never have."

He grabs me and drags me into the apartment. In a flash his lips are on mine and his body is pressed against me. I drop the keys, my bag, my phone and melt against him.

A flash of anger spikes inside me and I shove him away.

"No, wait, you don't get to kiss me and make me forget what I came here to say—" I stammer, trying to pull myself together.

"Actually, sweet girl, I get to do whatever the fuck I want. And that dress looks amazing on you by the way." He growls, coming at me again and lifting me off my feet, slamming me against the wall and wrapping one of my legs over his arm as he presses his cock between my legs.

CHAPTER TWENTY-EIGHT
Celso

Neve showing up at my door in that dress - it is exactly what I was hoping for. I have to admit that I didn't think I would get so lucky, but here she is.

And she has the cheek to stop me when I kiss her.

"No, wait, you don't get to kiss me and make me forget what I came here to say—" she stammers, stepping away from me. Swaying a little. Her sass is gorgeous. Her attitude is sexy. And I am going to break it right out of her and remind her who is in charge here.

"Actually, sweet girl, I get to do whatever the fuck I want. And that dress looks amazing on you by the way." I know what she came here for and I'm going to make sure she gets it.

It's not like I can control myself either way. I fucking want her. I need her. It's been way too long since I've tasted her lips on mine and it was so fucking hard to walk away from her, leaving her at the club with hundreds of men watching her.

I lift her in my arms, looping one arm beneath her knee and pushing her back against the wall. She gasps when I press my hips forward and let her feel how hard she makes me. Her legs are spread wide, her dress is hitched up over her hips and she couldn't escape even if she wanted to. But her eyes tell me what I need to know.

Oh - she's angry. She's up for a fight - but she wants this as much as I do.

I wrap my lips over hers and my fingers around her throat, pinning her down, doing what I've been craving.

She bites at my lip, and I jump, but I don't release her. Instead, my fingers around her throat tighten.

"Do you want me to punish you, angel? Because it won't be for your attitude tonight - it will be because you thought I would ever let you leave me." I snarl against her lips.

She takes a sharp breath and whispers in reply, "No one owns me, Celso. Not even you."

A low, dangerous growl rumbles up through my chest. She's wrong. She's so fucking wrong. I'll claim her like I did on our wedding night.

I step away from the wall with her still locked in my arms. I carry her to the kitchen counter.

Setting her down on it spins her around so that her back is facing me and she's kneeling on the cold marble. She tries to wiggle forward, away from me, so I grab her hips and drag her back towards me. Her legs are spread wide as she kneels, and I dip my fingers beneath her thin lace panties and rip them from her body. I pull her so that her ass is hanging off the edge of the counter and I push her face down.

Fuck, she's gorgeous. She's perfect.

And she's mine.

Her perfect light little pink pussy is begging for me to slam my cock into her.

She tries to wiggle away again, and I slap her ass. She screams and a red handprint burns into her pale, creamy skin.

"Move again and I'll make you cry." I warn her as I tug my pants open. My cock throbs, pulsing and twitching, desperate to be inside her.

I rub the tip of my cock across her pussy and moan deeply.

A little squeal of pleasure escapes her.

Grabbing her thighs I thrust forward. My cock plunging into her and pushing all the way inside her pussy, as deep as I can go as I grip her thighs and pull her back towards me.

She screams in pleasure and fright, her fingers gripping the edge of the counter.

I start to rock back and forth. Holding on to her because each time I thrust forward her entire body jolts.

Leaning forward I grab her throat from behind and pull her back against my chest as my cock continues to push inside her, stretching her wide open so that she can take all of me.

She starts to bounce on my cock, moaning with each movement.

My hands drift up her chest, I grab her dress and pull it down, freeing her breasts.

My fingers play around her nipples, tugging, pinching, and cupping her entire breast and she moans louder and moves faster on my cock.

She's so close to cuming.

My hand finds its way around her throat again and I lock her against me, not allowing her to move.

I fuck her so hard she is screaming. My cock is growing harder and bigger by the second.

"Wait." She cries out. "It's too big."

"You can handle me, angel. Just a little while longer." I growl against her ear as I plunge into her, over and over again. I slip my hand between her spread knees and rub my fingers over her clit, and she starts to shake. Now she's rocking her hips in small circles.

"Mm, fuck, you are so close. Stop fighting me." I demand.

She tilts her head back against me and shudders.

Her body clenches as muscles spasm and her pussy locks onto my cock.

The sensation of her cuming all over me causes me to fall over the edge and my orgasm explodes from me.

Neve stays leaning against me, my arm around her waist, her knees spread open and her head resting on my shoulder.

We are both breathing heavily, my cock still hard inside her.

I run my hand over her throat.

"I won't let you leave again." I whisper against her ear. "I've given you enough time away from me. Now you belong to me again."

I can sense the shift in her energy. She's smiling, I can tell without even looking at her.

"Is that so?" She smirks.

"That very much is so, my love."

I slide my cock out of her before it goes hard again.

I lift her off the counter and set her down on the ground. Picking up her torn panties I lift them to my face and breathe in the scent of her. Grinning at the expression of horror on her face. She reaches up and grabs them from me. "I've been dancing all night in those." she exclaims.

"Next time I'll let you dance on my face all night." I mutter, grabbing her close to me and kissing her.

"I'm serious, Neve. I won't let you go again."

She grins, her lips curving into a smile against mine. "It's ok. I don't think I want to go." She whispers.

"Are you serious? Don't mess with me on this. It won't turn out well." I say.

"I'm serious, Celso. I - I think I'm ready to come back."

"You still care about me? You want to be married to me?" I ask, worried she will say no, and that this is a trial.

Instead, she wraps her arms around my neck and stands on her tiptoes.

"I love you, asshole. I never stopped loving you I was - shocked. And angry. I might still be a little angry." She sighs.

I chuckle and she tilts her head to the side, narrowing her eyes at me. "What's funny about me being angry?" She asks.

"Well, if tonight is anything to go by - I think I might know how to sort you out whenever you get angry - and I think I might rather enjoy helping you let go of your anger."

She giggles as her cheeks flush pink.

"I can't complain about that—" she says, hiding her face against my chest.

I lift her chin and gaze into her eyes.

"I've missed you more than words can describe, Neve. I can't be without you. I'm a wreck without you. I need you in my life, by my side. I want my entire future to be *you*." I speak from the heart.

"I'm so scared you'll get bored with me after

you've realized I'm an ordinary girl - and you'll forget about me."

I crack up laughing because what she is suggesting is so ridiculously impossible, I don't know where to begin to explain this to her.

"My angel - you are anything but ordinary. And you and I are about to spend a lifetime together, going on every adventure we can dream up, experiencing the world together, learning about each other and every moment of every day - we are going to grow closer and more inseparable."

She smiles, a soft, beautiful smile that lights her eyes with glittering stars.

"I can't wait." She whispers.

"I love you, Neve. I always will." I whisper back to her.

I lift her in my arms and carry her to bed. I undress her slowly and she climbs beneath the blankets with me, her back curved against my chest. My arms locked around her, the scent of her hair on my pillow - everything is as it should be and for the first time in a very long time, I sleep deeply and peacefully.

In the morning Neve wakes up fresh and beautiful.

"No headache?" I ask, nuzzling my face into her neck with the blankets still wrapped warmly around us.

"No, and honestly, I'm surprised. Although it's been a while since I drank anything, so I think I got tipsy off a minimal amount of shots." She laughs.

"You were a little more than tipsy, my love."

She huffs. "Don't be so dramatic." She laughs, turning around and nuzzling against my chest.

I sigh. I still have to ask.

"Last night, you were a little drunk, and I know that might have affected the choices you made. I need to ask you again—"

"Yes." She says, interrupting me.

"What?" I stammer, confused.

"Yes, Celso. I am madly in love with you. Yes, I want to move back in here. Yes, I want to spend the rest of my life with you and yes, I want to be married to you."

She grins, her gorgeous blue eyes looking at me with mischief. "Did I leave anything out? Because I can carry on."

"Oh, can you? What else?" I ask, smirking.

"Yes, you are the hottest guy I've ever seen in my life. Yes, when you touch me it's like a drug, I can't get enough of. Yes, you make me the happiest I've ever been in my life. Yes, your cock is—" I kiss her. She's laughing against my lips as I press my mouth over hers and pull her body to lie on top of mine.

Our kiss grows deeper, more intimate and my heart tightens in my chest. When she tilts her head away, she is smiling with a more serious expression. "I mean it, Celso. I love you. I love you. All I want is to be with you. I tried to stay away. I was scared and worried about what you'd done, but I don't care. None of it matters. I want to be with you."

"That's all I need to hear, my angel. I love you too. And all I want is you."

CHAPTER TWENTY-NINE
Neve

The morning after clubbing with Dalila I wake up in Celso's bed - my bed - and I'm happy. We talk for ages. I let out everything that was in my heart - my fears and what I want for the future, even though I don't really know - I am sure I want trust and honesty and openness. I want to rely on him.

We talk and we listen late in the morning. We are still curled up in each other's arms when Celso says, "I'll give you a lift to your brother's place so you can fetch all your things. You're moving back in today. I won't spend another night without my wife by my side."

A thought strikes me, and I scrunch my nose as I prop myself up onto my elbows and stare at him. "Why did you ignore me?" I ask. "For the last few days, you didn't even message me. Why?"

He chuckles.

"To be honest, there are two reasons. The first is that I thought you needed some proper space to think clearly without me breathing down your neck."

I narrow my eyes. "And the second?"

"I thought I'd let you see what it is like to miss me and realize what you're giving up?" I chuckle.

I push him playfully on the arm. "You are so freaking cheeky." I mutter.

He grabs me and rolls me over, his body over mine as he presses me into the mattress, pinned beneath him.

"But you came running - so it worked." He says seductively.

"Came running?" I exclaim. "Excuse me?"

He laughs at the warmth of it rolls through me, swelling in my heart and making me smile. "Fine. I came running. Especially when you left the club as though I meant nothing."

"What you don't know is that I've been watching you the whole time. Even while I was silent. I never took my eyes off you."

The thrill of his words runs through me, and I spread my legs, wrapping them around him.

He growls low and deep and presses his lips over mine.

By late afternoon I am moved back in and unpacked. You should have seen my brother's face when he saw Celso was there to help me fetch my things. I've never seen someone looking more relieved than he looked today.

It still bothers me - that he cares so much about his campaign and so little about whether or not I am happy. But at the end of the day all I need is one person who will go to the end of the earth and back for me. And I have him.

Somehow, across the millions of people on this planet, I got lucky enough to find the person who makes me happy.

He has proven to me how far he will go to win my heart and how far he will go to keep me. He is my world, and I am his and I don't doubt that for a second.

I zip my empty suitcase up and stand on my tiptoes to slide it onto the top shelf of the bedroom cupboards. Celso steps up behind me and takes it from my hand, easily putting it away. My body tingles with him standing so close to me. He runs his hands over my waist and kisses my neck.

"You're packing this away, but in no time at all I'll be taking it down for you again." He chuckles.

"I will?"

"Come on, I'll show you how far I got."

"With what?"

He led me to the dining room, across the whole table there are brochures spread out. Along with a map. On the map there are red and blue dotted lines he has marked out with thick pens.

"What is this?" I ask, my body filling with excitement.

"This is a map of Peru, and this is a map of Cambodia, to Vietnam. I've plotted routes for us. The red line is easy travel. We can catch a bus or a train or something like that. The blue lines are where we have to fly, either by plane or helicopter. Some places are so remote you can't get there any other way. Then these thinner blue lines are boat trips."

"You've planned everything?" I say, my mouth dropping open at the intricacy of it all.

"I wanted something off the track, away from the tourist traps. We would backpack, traveling light, hiking through places that most people never even dream of seeing."

"This is incredible, Celso." I whisper, touching my fingertips over the routed adventure.

"All you have to decide is if you want to go to Peru, and Mexico, or if you want to go to Asia. Of course, whichever one you choose now - we can do the other one later in the year - but our honeymoon is going to be something we remember forever. So, you decide - "

He sits down and pulls me onto his lap. He drags a few of the brochures in front of me.

"These are the touristy places, but the photos and venues - it gives you an idea of the type of holiday. And of course, we might stay in some hotels in between our rougher side of the trip. We might need a break from the jungle and a hot tub and a cocktail." He laughs.

I reach out and touch both brochures. Both trips would be incredible, but there is something about those jungles in Asia that are calling to me.

"This one." I say pulling the Asian brochure closer.

"I'll start booking the flights. I've already made a list of things for you to pack after I did some research. We can leave as soon as you like."

"Are you serious? You want to go on such a wild adventure with me?" I ask.

"My angel, I've been waiting for you - so that we can go on these types of adventures together. You and me - we're the same in so many ways. We both want this freedom. This escape from the norm. And now we get to do it together."

I turn to kiss him, hugging him.

I could not have asked for a more perfect man.

The night before we leave for our honeymoon, Dalila and Nevio come for dinner.

I'm excited, over excited, and talking nonstop about all the incredible things we are going to see.

Dalila sits at the dining room table, our takeaway pizza boxes are open, and everyone is helping themselves to whatever they want. The guys are talking about four-by-four vehicles and what would be the best one to invest in. Dalila nudges me under the table with her foot.

"You're glowing, Neve. It's so nice to see you smiling like this."

"I'm so happy, Dalila. I can't describe it."

"You don't need to. It's written all over your face. My brother too - he's like a neon glow stick he's glowing so much." She laughs. "You guys were made for each other, huh?" She shrugs.

"I'm going to be sending you photos the entire trip." I tell her, sipping my drink.

"By the looks of things, you guys will not have signal in most of the places you're going. Just make sure you don't get bitten by some weird spider and come back with superpowers. I just want my friend back - in one piece." She smirks. "But here is to an amazing honeymoon, doing what your heart desires." She lifts her glass to me.

Celso overhears the last part of our conversation.

"To our adventure, my love." He smiles, lifting his glass too.

Nevio chuckles. "To finding the perfect person who makes you smile every day." He says his eyes on Dalila. Dalila grins and scrunches her nose.

I'm so happy that she has accepted our relationship - and that we can still be best friends. It would have broken my heart to lose her, but I see now that the people who are meant to be in our lives find a way of staying, even when things get complicated or difficult. Dalila is meant to be my friend.

Celso is my forever person.

We always land up where we are meant to be in the world. And I am meant to be right here. With him.

I stare across the table at Celso and my heart warms. He smiles, the most gorgeous smile that shows off his dimples. His perfect jaw and those bright blue eyes.

He is mine and I am his and that is how it's meant to be.

In the morning, I wake up before the sun rises.

I'm alert, far too excited to do anything but leap out of bed.

Celso grabs my arm and pulls me back towards him before I do so.

"Wait, you aren't getting away yet." He laughs, holding me against him.

"I have so much to do." I giggle, wiggling in his grip.

"No, you don't. I've done it all for you. Everything is arranged. I helped you pack already. You literally only have to get dressed and climb into the plane."

I grin. "Alright, well, I'm too excited not to do anything, so what do you suggest I do to distract myself." I huff.

"I have something specific in mind." He chuckles, his hand running down my back.

CHAPTER THIRTY
Celso

Neve is giggling with excitement as we board my private jet. The air hostess leads us to our seats and brings us two glasses of champagne. "Happy honeymoon." She smiles, leaving us to enjoy the golden liquid while we wait for take-off.

Neve can't sit still. She's wiggling in her seat, up and down, looking out the window, leaning against me, talking nonstop.

I love seeing her like this. She's so happy.

It's a long flight to Sihanoukville airport in Cambodia. Eventually I get her to settle down and sleep a little because I want her to arrive fresh and not jet lagged.

We land in the quiet, rural town of Sihanoukville in the early hours of the morning.

The people are friendly and down to earth. We catch a tuktuk, our backpacks on our backs, to the beach villa we are staying in for the first two nights while we establish ourselves and enjoy a day or two of relaxation.

We are staying right on the beach, our back door leads directly onto the white sandy beaches and in the late afternoon locals come past with trays of fresh seafood which we can buy and cook fresh for ourselves.

If we don't want to cook, there are little beach restaurants, tables in the sand, that serve massive platters of prawns and calamari, drenched in butter and accompanied by cocktails in coconut shells.

At night we lie out on the wooden deck listening to the waves crash against the shore.

"I can't wait for tomorrow." Neve says. She hasn't stopped smiling since we arrived.

"It's a long walk, the first day. Our jungle guide is going to drop us at the first stop and go to a nearby village until morning. We'll be alone in the middle of the jungle."

"It's so exciting." She grins wiggling in my arms. "Do you think that on the way back we can visit the village and spend a night with the locals?"

"I'm sure they'd be happy to show us their home." I say, leaning down to kiss her.

Over the next five days we hike through jungles, up rivers that never end, swimming with massive fish that nibble at our arms and legs and make Neve scream. We see entire bushes covered in butterflies that all flutter away when we shake the leaves. We find elephants roaming free and calm deep in the jungles. We meet native people along the way and share food with them.

We stand underneath massive, heavy waterfalls and let the streams pound against our bodies.

At night we sleep beneath a sky full of stars, or under a tent made of mesh to keep the bugs out. We smell like earth and salt and fresh air.

Our skin is tanned, and our smiles are wider than ever before.

About a week into our adventure, I have a surprise waiting for Neve at our next camp.

We arrive early in the afternoon and Neve gasps when she sees the cabin, a hot tub, an outdoor shower, and an outdoor fire pit. The cabin is simple, but luxurious compared to the last few days.

Our guide leaves us for the night, smiling and bowing before he makes his way to his own site.

"This is sneaky." Neve giggles, dumping her backpack at the door of the cabin. We go inside and they prepared the place as I asked them to.

There is fresh fruit, food for us to cook on the open flames, custard cakes for dessert, candles everywhere and a bottle of champagne.

Outside they have already started the fire that heats the tub and there are rose petals floating in the scented water.

"Let's soak for a while, afterwards we can make some food." I suggest.

Neve doesn't wait - she strips her clothes off.

I chuckle and start doing the same. Fresh air against my skin is amazing. Neve looks like a wild child as she steps out of the cabin, into the jungle, wearing nothing at all.

We soak all afternoon, the water staying warm because of the fire and our muscles loving the heat. Between the trees above us the stars come out and the moon shines bright and full.

Neve drifts over to me in the water.

"Celso." She says. "This is better than I could ever have dreamed it would be."

"I wouldn't want to be here with anyone else in the entire world." I grin. "One day we will be telling our grandchildren about this."

She tilts her head to the side. "You want kids?" she asks, surprised. I pull her close to me, letting her lie in the hot water with her back against my chest and my legs wrapped on either side of her. We both stare up towards the night sky.

"If you do. I am happy either way. We can have a massive family, or it can be you and me forever. But if we have kids, it'll only be later, after a ton of these adventures."

"I agree." She grins, snuggling against me. "We have so much time to decide these things. It's so amazing to not have the future set in stone, to have options, to choose any direction."

"Any direction as long as we are together." I reach over the edge of the tub and pick up the small wooden box I've been carrying around with me. Waiting for this moment.

I set it down on her stomach and it floats a little in the water.

"What is this?" She asks, picking it up.

"Open it." I whisper. My heart is beating fast. I'm nervous even though I'm sure I know what she will say when I ask. I made the choice to ask this time. I want her to choose this. Last time there was no choice, and I forced the situation and until I ask her, I will always wonder about it.

Neve is quiet for a moment as she stares at the little box, she turns it in her fingers, brushing her fingers over the textured surface.

She lifts the lid open and inside she finds the most exquisite diamond ring, crafted especially for her, glittering as wildly as the stars around us.

I hear her take a sharp breath, but she doesn't get as excited as I thought she would. Perhaps she doesn't understand what I am doing—that I am asking her this time.

"Celso?" she asks, confused.

"Will you marry me, my angel?" I say through a wide grin.

"We are already married—" she says.

"Will you marry me again?" I chuckle. "Will you be my wife, again? We can have a wedding on the beach here in Cambodia. Just you and me. Saying our vows together. You can wear whatever you want, and we can dance beneath the moon."

She turns in the tub and sits up, her legs wrapped around my waist as she straddles me. Her eyes are filled with hunger and love. A craving deep inside her she needs fulfilled.

My body responds instantly. All she has to do is look at me in that way and my cock swells, growing rock hard beneath her.

She lifts the ring from the box and slips it onto her finger. "I will marry you, a thousand times, over and over again in this life and in every life, I live after this one. I will find you in every one of them." She leans forward and presses her lips against mine.

I push my cock inside her. Her pussy is warm and tight, and she rocks her hips back and forth as she rides me out in the wild jungle night.

We move together, savoring the pleasure of being with each other.

My cock is throbbing and pulsing, desperate to have every inch of her, to consume her in every way.

Neve tilts her head back and looks up at the stars as she rides me, her hand pressed against my chest, her ring shining.

I will marry her a thousand times in a thousand lifetimes too.

She is moaning into the still air. The sound of it bounces off the trees around us and somewhere nearby an animal scrambles away in fright.

I grab her hips and start moving her faster, splashing water over the edge of the tub, not caring at all.

Her pussy tightens on me as she changes pace, dancing, rolling her hips in a circular motion.

"Fuck, you are so perfect my angel." I growl, struggling to control myself.

"Let's disappear forever." She whispers. Staring down at me with those bright blue eyes. Full of mystery and adventure. Full of mischief and mayhem. She is the perfect girl for me.

She is my everything. She is my entire world.

Neve leans forward and wraps her hand around my throat. She grins at me.

Tonight, she is letting her darker side out, and it's driving me crazy.

She tightens her fingers around my throat and while I can feel it, I can sense the power it's giving her.

I smirk, knowing she is a kitten in my hands, but letting her sink her teeth into me, nonetheless.

She rides me harder, rocking back and forth as my cock moves inside her.

She moans louder. The most beautiful sound in all the world.

I can sense she is close to cuming, but now it's my turn to take her.

Sitting up I wrap my arm around her back and grab her hair from behind, tilting her head back and exposing her neck. I lift her and start slamming my cock into her. Over and over again.

She screams in delight as I fill her up, pushing so deep inside her I can see her stomach moving. She grabs the edge of the bath and brings her legs forward over my shoulders.

I keep fucking her, harder and harder, pushing myself into her and watching her expression drift in waves of pleasure.

When her orgasm hits her - her feet tighten around my neck, her legs shaking against my chest.

I explode inside her at the same time, the sight of her pleasure is my pleasure.

Neve lets out a heavy, satisfied breath of laughter.

"Wow." She giggles.

I pull her up, back onto my lap.

"I think I'm ready to eat everything in the cabin now." I laugh.

"Me too. Wow." She says again. Then she glances at her hand, spreading her fingers and wiggling them so she can admire the ring and how it sparkles when she moves it.

She bites her bottom lip, her eyes welling up with tears.

"Neve, what's wrong?" I ask.

"I'm so happy." She mutters, a whisper as her throat closes over her words. "I'm - so freaking happy." She says again, and grabs me around my neck and hugs me, the entire world wouldn't be able to pull us apart.

"It's you and me, my love. You and me against the world."

About the Author

Hannah Rio is from a small town where she grew up reading romance books sent monthly by her book club. She developed a flair for crafting intricate love stories. She understands the delicate dance of heartbreak and joy. As a storyteller, she enjoys contemporary romances with strong, ambitious leading characters working through life's unexpected twists. Her female and male characters can make hearts flutter and eyes tear up. Her novels promise to bring readers back to continue events of new love and passion, secrets, surprises, painful memories, sassy and sweet, grumpy or good-hearted, and adventures with happy ever after endings.

**Sign up to her newsletter here:
subscribepage.io/NKn98Z**

Also by Hannah Rio

BILLIONAIRES & BABY DADDY'S

His Surprise Baby

Billionaire Baby Daddy Dilemma

Off-Limits Silver Fox Boss

Mistle-Tied To My Silver Fox Boss

MAFIA MEN

Vece Familia Series

Claiming His Mafia Princess

Something Old

Something New

Something Borrowed

Something Blue

A Six Pence For You Shoe

<u>Shattered Revenge - A Vece, Rivas crossover novella</u>

Shattered Pieces Dark Mafia Series (Coming 2025)

King

Queen

Bishop

Knight

Rook

Pawn

HANNAH RIO

Printed in Great Britain
by Amazon